I0545299

A Week's Worth of Fiction
Volumes 1 &2 Paperback Edition

A Week's Worth of Fiction Volume 1
People of The Edge

Stories, Lyrics and Poems by Mark Wilkins

Livin' on The Edge
The Terror
When Will We Learn to Communicate?
The Butterfly
Big City Girl
The Old One
Unique
The Boba Banana Saga
Dream Street
Welcome to the Circus
Dark Thoughts
The Mercy Date
Powerless
Safety First
A Silent Scream
How The Poems in this Volume are Related to the Stories

A Week's Worth of Fiction 2
Science Fiction Stories

Stories, Lyrics & Poems by Mark Wilkins

Robot Chickens
Sincerity

Barter World
Rat Race
Mr. Boston's First Day
Escape
Precious Liquid
Lost Between Two Worlds
The Juice Fly
Everyday Heroes
Her Rash
Get Me Through The Night
The Highway Fire
Freedom
How The Poems in This Book are related to The Stories

In Volume 1 of A Week's Worth of Fiction, you will meet people on the edges of society. A security guard who struggles with an imminent death, an elderly man whose cast aside and left to die, one woman struggling to capture romance before her beauty fades and another struggling with cancer. You will meet a little boy who terrorizes a grocery store, a teenage boy searching for love and a small nation struggling against a corporate monopoly. If you want fictional stories you will never forget you only need to count to 7.

Volume 2 of A Week's Worth of Fiction includes stories of Science Fiction. Within its pages you will meet stories about a girl who has the cure for a deadly disease, a woman on a date with psycho somatic disease called prophecy, a robot chicken, a supernatural fly, an astral projection, a teacher in a new job where everything is not what it seems and a futuristic world where the only economy is barter. If you want science fiction stories you will never forget you only need to count to 7.

All Contents Copyright 1979, 1980, 1981, 1982, 1983, 1985, 1987, 1989, 1990, 1993, 1994, 1996, 1997, 1998, 2010, 2011, 2012, 2013, 2014, 2015, 2016, 2017, 2018, Loveforce International Publishing Company. All Rights Reserved.

What is A Week's Worth of Fiction?

This book is part of a series of books called A Week's Worth of Fiction. The series is called A Week's Worth of Fiction for two reasons. First, there are seven stories in each book to mirror the seven days of a week. Second, each book in the series is part of an exciting new concept. Although you could read the entire book as a short read, we suggest you try reading just one story a day for a week. This will give you the experience of living with each story for a day. It is by living with each story for a day that you can think about it. Thinking about it could reveal subtle nuances contained in the story that will deliver deep insight into what each story means for you.

Each story is followed by a poem. The poem relates to the story but it is up to you, the reader, to determine how it's related to the story. Sometimes the poem is there to make a commentary about the situation the character is in. Other times it's to provide a clue into the life of a character. Still other times it's there to provide an opportunity to explore a concept indirectly related to the concept of the story. Thinking about the story and the poem that comes after it will give you food for thought and provide a different insight into the story from the different nuances that the poem brings to your understanding of it. Living with the story and the poem that follows it, is a unique concept developed by us, as a publisher for you, the reader.

Each book in the A Week's Worth of Fiction series explores a different concept. Volume one explores People on The Edge. All of the stories are centered on people on the margins of society who are often in desperate circumstances. Volume two, Science Fiction, contains stories that explore various science fiction themes. Volume 3 The Many Faces of Violence explores stories which include characters who are involved with various acts of violence. Volume 4, Realizations involve characters who come to an epiphany of one sort or another. This A Week's Worth of Fiction book, is part of a series of fiction books by Mark Wilkins. A Week's Worth of Fiction is also part of a larger series of books called the A Storyteller Book Series. Other series of books in the A Storyteller Series include Stories of The Supernatural (Occult-Horror), Slices of Life (Humor), and Classroom Confessions (Stories about students & teachers).

We hope that you will enjoy this book as well as other books in this series and other books we publish. We strive to deliver new and novel experiences for readers and publish e-books in many different genres.

Sincerely,

The Friendly Folks at Love Force International Publishing

Living on the Edge

Don't know what to do
Don't know what to say
When I hear dreams of past generations
Are coming true today

So many miracles
It can boggle one's mind
But what good are miracles that don't
Solve the problems that we have in our lives?

I keep hearing about
Improvements in the economy
But I wonder when
They'll be filtering down to me

Cause I'm living on the edge
The fine line between luck and disaster
Yes, I'm living on the edge
Hanging on with all that I've got

When you're living on the edge
You've got to be extra careful
Cause when living on the edge
So many things can push you right off

I've got hope

Deep inside
It's the light that dispels the darkness
The darkness that would leave me blind

And I've got the patience
To hang tough and endure
Cause there's changes on the horizon
That'll make things better for sure

But anger and despair
Keep trying to break into my heart
And the battle to keep them out
Is tearing me apart!

Cause I'm living on the edge
The fine line between luck and disaster
Yes, I'm living on the edge
Hanging on with all that I've got

When you're living on the edge
You've got to be extra careful
Cause when living on the edge
So many things can push you right off

The Terror

He saw the Terror when he first entered the department store. The Terror was with his weary, single mother and frightened younger brothers. At just four years old, the terror wanted desperately to get his way. His mother dreaded taking him anywhere but none of her relatives would watch him and she didn't dare leave him alone with a babysitter. The Terror was yelling and kicking at the shopping cart while his mother and brothers stood looking at him, powerless to do anything about his rage.

"You better give me the toy I want!" He demanded. "You better give it to me or you'll be sorry!" He continued.

The man went about his shopping and didn't give the terror a second thought. He walked over to the checkout lines when he finished a half an hour later. He was dismayed to find that there was a long line at each of the six cash registers. The exit door was about 50 feet to the right of the sixth cash register. He decided to get in line at the first register, the farthest from the exit door because that line was about two people shorter than all the other lines. Within seconds, he heard a familiar sound.

"Get me my toy! Get it!"

He looked over to where the noise was coming from and two registers over, close to the front of the line he saw The Terror yelling. His beleaguered mother tried to calm him down. Many of the people in the checkout lines were looking at The Terror and the commotion he was making.

"It's okay sweetie, we'll get you a toy next time." She said calmly.

This bit of news angered The Terror.

"Next time?" He questioned. "No! I want it NOW!!"

The Terror began whining and crying and kicking the shopping cart furiously in a tantrum.

"Why can't I have the toy? Why? I want it NOW!!!!" He screamed at a pitch so high some of the people in the lines had to put their hands over their ears.

With that particular scream, literally everyone in all of the checkout lines began looking at The Terror and his mother.

"Now dear, we don't have enough money to get you a toy this time." She said in a calm voice.

The Terror's eyes seemed to enlarge. He began screaming.

"I hate you! I HATE YOU! You are the worst mommy in the whole world! I'm never going to forgive you! I'll hate you for this forever! Do you hear me? Forever!!!!" He screamed as he tantrumed and cried simultaneously.

This went on for the five minutes that the mother and her children waited in line to pay for their things. During the course of the five minutes, people waiting in not only her checkout line, but all of the checkout lines began staring at them with angry disgust. Some of them began muttering to themselves and others began talking about it. They said things like:

"Why doesn't she just smack that brat?"

"Doesn't she have any consideration for others?"

"Why does she even take that kid in public?"

"She should have left that brat a t home."

"Why doesn't she just leave her crap in the cart and leave the store?"

Then the mother got up to the register. She paid for her things as the cashier loaded them into her shopping cart. Just as she was about to roll out of the store, The Terror laid down in the middle of the floor. She told him to get up but he refused. He began kicking and screaming.

"I'm not going anywhere until I get my toy! You can't make me go. You are a bad mommy! BAD MOMMY!!!!" He yelled between kicks.

It was three long minutes of listening to the tantrum before the man got up to the cash register. In those minutes, people who checked out voiced their disapproval to the mother as they left. The poor mother turned red with embarrassment. Seeing his mother turn red emboldened The Terror, who in turn, kicked and screamed even louder while lying on the floor.

"Stay here and do that all you want, I am still not buying that toy for you!" She yelled back at him.

In response, The Terror began weeping loudly and uncontrollably.

Having paid for his things, the man began walking towards the exit. Instead of shuffling past The Terror as everyone else did, he stopped next to him and began to talk to the boy's mother.

"May I talk to your son?" He asked.

"Why do you want to talk to him?" She replied.

"I think I might be able to calm him down." He said.

"You're not going to hit him are you?" She asked.

"No." He replied.

"Or yell at him?" She asked.

"No, I'm just going to talk to him calmly, as you do." He replied.

"Good luck with that." She said. "Sometimes he stays like this for a couple of hours." She added.

"What's the boy's name?" The man asked.

"Bobby." His mother replied.

The man walked over to the boy so that he was towering directly above him. Then he calmly called the boy's name.

"Bobby." He said.

The boy ignored him. The boy's mother gave the man a look that if translated into words, would have said "I told you so." Undeterred, the man looked down at the boy.

"Is that you Bobby?" He a bit louder said in a calm tone of voice.

The boy looked up at the man.

"Do I know you?" He asked the man.

"I live down the street from you Bobby and I always thought you were a very smart boy!" The man stated.

"I am smart." Bobby replied confidently.

"Oh, I agree with you Bobby, really I do, but you see all of these people Bobby?" He said as he pointed towards the people in the checkout lines.

Bobby looked up at all of the people in the checkout lines. He saw the anger and scowls of disapproval on their faces.

"Those people?" Asked Bobby.

"Yes those people." The man replied. "Well, they all think that you are not smart at all." The man continued.

"Why?" Asked Bobby.

"Well, you have been screaming and crying and carrying on for a long time now, and, do you have the toy you want Bobby?" The man asked.

"No." Replied Bobby.

"It seems to me Bobby that a smart boy would see that this isn't working for him and try something different. Are you a smart boy Bobby?" The man said.

"I am smart!" Bobby stated emphatically with a whine in his voice.

"Then Bobby…" The man said. "Why don't you try something different?"

"Like what?" Asked Bobby.

"First, let's get up off of the floor, shall we? I'll help you up." The man said as he extended his hand to Bobby.

Bobby grabbed onto the man's hand. The man lifted Bobby up as easily as a child can lift a feather. Once Bobby was up on his feet, he looked at the man.

"Now what?" Asked Bobby.

"First, you must earn the respect of all the people who are looking at you." The man said.

"How do I do that?" Bobby asked.

"By telling them you are sorry for not acting like the smart boy that you really are." He said.

"I can't do that!" Bobby replied.

"Sure you can Bobby and when you do, you can see how your words magically affect all of them." The man said.

"Magic?" Bobby asked.

"Yes Bobby, because words have power. The words you said before had the power to make all of these people upset with you but saying you are sorry will have the power to change the looks on their faces." The man said instructionally.

Bobby looked at all of the people in the checkout lines.

"I'm sorry." He said.

The looks on everyone's faces changed from anger to forgiveness.

'Wow!!!" Exclaimed Bobby with shocked joy.

Then he looked at the man again.

"Now what?" Bobby asked again.

"Now you must say you are sorry to your mommy and brothers so you can see the magic work on them too." The man said.

"I'm sorry mommy, you really are a good mommy." Bobby said.

Then he hugged his two brothers while saying "Sorry guys."

As Bobby apologized to his siblings, his mother looked up at the man and mouthed "He's never apologized to me before." The man turned to leave. He began to walk towards the store exit. Bobby, sensing that the man was leaving, called out to him.

"Hey mister!" Bobby shouted.

The man turned around.

"What about my toy?" He asked. "How do I get it?" He continued.

The man walked back over to Bobby.

"When was the last time you acted like you did earlier and actually got a toy?" He asked.

"I think I was two." Bobby replied after pausing to think about the question.

'So now, if you want to get a toy, try being a good boy and doing everything your mommy tells you to do and maybe you will get a toy *sometimes*." The man said.

"Sometimes?" Asked Bobby with a hint of anger in his voice.

"Yes." Said the man. "But sometimes is less time to wait than two years is. You will get what you want more often by being a good boy, at least that's what a smart boy would do and aren't you a smart boy Bobby?"

"I am a smart boy." Bobby replied happily.

When Will We Learn to Communicate?

Congested traffic
Hustle bustle
Migraine headaches
Aching muscles
Crowded sidewalks
Pushing, shoving
We're too busy
To spend time loving

When will we learn to communicate?
When will we finally
Learn to communicate
On a humanistic level?
When will we communicate?

People saying
What they're not meaning
Double talking
Petty scheming
Phony faces
Masquerading
No one really
Communicating

When will we learn to communicate?

Prejudicial

Olden timers
Shrewd and ruthless
Social climbers
Plastic people
Never sharing
No one reaching
No one caring

When will we learn to communicate?

The Butterfly

It was New Year's Eve. He was at the nightclub alone. He had seen women like her before. She was a butterfly. He was immediately attracted to her but he didn't really know why. She was a beautiful Latina. Tall, dark skinned, curvy with large breasts and a firm, round ass. He knew she would be attracted to him, butterflies always were.

He watched her for a bit. She seemed to be there alone as well. There were guys interested in her but none of them had made a move. He walked up to her.

"Hi, my name is Marco, what's yours?" He asked.

"Selena." She replied.

He looked at the drink she had in her hand. It was almost empty.

"What's that you're drinking?" He asked her.

"It's called Melon Ball." She replied.

Marco immediately visualized himself balling her melons. He wasn't sure if she was just being sexually suggestive or if there actually was a drink called Melon Ball. Risking possible embarrassment, he motioned to the waitress. The waitress walked over to them.

"Two melon balls please." He asked.

"Have you ever has one before?" Selena asked.

"No, but I'm willing to try anything once." He replied

"My kind of guy!" She exclaimed.

And so began a night of drunken debauchery. She ended up going home with him and they made like bunny rabbits having wild sex in every room in his one bedroom apartment. In between the sex, they talked. Selena seemed impressed by how intelligent and worldly Marco was. He completed college and had traveled all over the world. She told him she wanted to get to know him better.

Every time Marco asked Selena about her life, she just gazed in the other direction, misty eyed. He kept pressing her about why she seemed so sad but she resisted him until she could see the first rays of the sun coming up.

"I have a husband and five children." She finally uttered.

Marco's whole composure changed. He got serious.

"Why aren't you with them?" He asked.

"My husband thinks I'm an ugly pig and he hasn't touched me sexually for years. My children are at a sleepover. I needed to get out and get laid, you know, just to maintain my sanity." She confided.

Marco sat and thought for a minute. He enjoyed being with Selena. He really enjoyed the sex but he had never been with a married woman before and he had reservations about that. Then again, her husband hadn't touched her in years so perhaps he didn't care what she did sexually. Selena sensed that Marco was conflicted.

"You know, honey, I've been with other men before, you aren't the first. My husband knows this and he doesn't care." She said.

A look of relief settled upon Marco's face.

"You know baby, I thought this was just going to be a one night stand, but you are so worldly and wise. I've never met anyone like you before. I think we could be, not boyfriend and girlfriend, more like friends with benefits. All I ask is that you teach me. Teach me by telling me about your experiences in other countries, expose me to other cultures and new concepts. I want you to help me grow as a person." She continued.

For the next couple of months, Selena would get together with Marco whenever she could. He worked during the day so they only went out at night. Selena didn't have a car, so Marco would pick her up a couple of blocks from her house. He took Selena to art exhibits, cultural events and all kinds of foreign restaurants. He would tell her about the places he had traveled, things he had learned in his college classes and anything else she wanted to hear about. Once in a while they would go out clubbing and sometimes they would bring Selena's girlfriend Rachel, a tall, thin, beautiful Native American woman, along. The nights always ended back at his apartment with a few drinks and sex.

Then on Valentine's Day night, Marco took Selena and Rachel out to a night club. As soon as they got there, Selena and Rachel went to the ladies room. Marco went to the bar. It took him about 20 minutes to finish his first drink. He still didn't see Selena and Rachel. He decided to walk around the club and find them.

As he walked through the club he saw Jacqueline, a tall, curvy Latina he once dated years before. He walked up to her to say hello. Jaqueline introduced Marco to her husband Mario. They ended up talking for a half an hour. Early in the conversation, Marco had described Selena and Rachel and what they were wearing. Suddenly, Mario tapped Marco on the shoulder.

"Hey bro, aren't those the two girls you described?" He said.

Marco turned around and saw Selena grinding and kissing on another guy right out on the dance floor. He saw Rachel doing the same thing.

"You gonna let that guy bump and grind on your girlfriend bro?" Mario asked.

"She's not my girlfriend, she's just a friend." Marco said in a shamefully transparent attempt to save face.

Marco walked over to Selena. She looked up and saw him coming. She whispered something into the ear of the guy she was grinding with and walked over to meet Marco.

"I thought you were here with me!" Marco stated angrily.

"Not really," Selena said. "We just needed a ride but we'll be going home with these guys tonight. "

Shock and anger hit across Marcos face like it was slapped by a hurricane force wind. He wanted to hit Selena but he would never hit a woman. He did the only thing he could do to avoid letting anger get the better of him. He turned and stormed out of the club. He took his anger out by speeding down the freeway and driving erratically.

All the way home he was thinking about how Selena had betrayed him. How she treated him like a chauffeur and a punk using him for a ride and then ditching him at the club after he paid her way in. He thought about how she had embarrassed him in front of Jaqueline and her husband, who he could never talk to again out of the shame stemming from this night.

Over the next several days, both Selena and Rachel called him. He let the calls go straight to the voice mail. They both left apologetic messages. They both tried to get Marco to go out with them. Marco listened to the messages but he didn't respond.

Then, one day, Rachel said something that made him change his mind about her. She said that he didn't really have a relationship with her and that he had no reason to be mad at her. After thinking about it, Marco realized that she was right. He called her back and they began dating. They dated off and on for four months. One day, in mid-June, Marco casually asked about Selena.

"You wouldn't recognize her." Rachel said. "She put on about forty six pounds." She continued.

"I know." Said Marco. "Her metamorphosis was short lived this time, wasn't it?" He asked.

Rachel just looked at him with a confused look on her face.

"Selena is a butterfly isn't she?" Marco asked.

"A, What?" Rachel replied, still confused.

"A butterfly, a person who has a weight problem, who is normally grossly overweight. Every now and then they go on a diet that works and they become thinner. They emerge like a butterfly from the cocoon of fat they have been encased in for so long. They spread their wings and fly, realizing that they are suddenly attractive, reveling in the attention and trying to compress a lifetime of pleasure into a short time because they know it will be only a short time before they put the weight back on and go back into their cocoon and hibernate." Marco explained.

It took a few moments for Rachel to absorb the gravity of what Marco said. Then she spoke.

"That's Selena exactly! She works out like a demon, loses a lot of weight, realizes men are attracted to her again and parties like there's no tomorrow. Then she gains the weight back, men are no longer attracted and she settles back into the boringness of her life." She said.

Marco called Rachel the next week but her number had been disconnected. He went by her apartment but the landlord said they moved. Something inside told him that he would never see or hear from Rachel again.

It was The Fourth of July. He was at the nightclub alone. He had seen women like her before. She was a butterfly. He was immediately attracted to her but he didn't really know why. She was a beautiful African American woman, Tall, dark skinned, curvy with large breasts and a firm, round ass. He knew she would be attracted to him, butterflies always were.

Big City Girl

VERSE 1
She used to go out rock & rollin'
All night long
But now she's got a couple of children
One's just a babe in arms
She wanted to be a movie star
Then settled for settling down
But the man she chose didn't work out right
And now he ain't even around
CHORUS
She's a big city girl
Or is she a woman?
Big city girl
She's a big city girl
Turning into an old woman
Big city girl
VERSE 2
Men, they come a driftin'
In and out of her life
Sometimes one stays longer
Than just a couple of nights
When they tell her she's been liberated
She doesn't know what they mean
Cause the only good jobs she can get
Are the ones that are in her dreams
(repeat chorus)

VERSE 3
She's barely into her twenties
And the wrinkles have started to set
No matter how close she comes to it
She can never quite get out of debt
She tries to blame it on the system
But her friends tell her it's just the times
And she curses at the things that hold her back
After all, she's still in her prime
(repeat chorus)

You can hear this song by googling bandcamp and once on bandcamp, typing in the loveforce collective.

The Old One

Kallah had first heard about the Walk with The Ancestors Ritual when he was a young boy. His great grandfather had told Kallah that he would soon take that walk. A few weeks later, when Kallah's grandfather had reached his 60th birthday, he put on good animal skin pants, a shirt, a warm jacket and a knapsack with some food in it. He said goodbye to his family and the others in the tribe and walked into the Great Forrest. He was never seen again.

Kallah's father explained that the Walk with The Ancestors Ritual was a necessary part of the circle of life. He explained that his tribe lived in a clearing in the middle of The Great Forrest and that that clearing had limited space. In order to make room for the strong and healthy, the old had to leave the tribe on their 60th birthday. They had walk West out into the Great Forrest until they meet their ancestors in the great beyond where no living person had ever gone.

As the years passed, Kallah grew strong. He became a great hunter and fisherman. He was a great warrior as well. He had felled many a deer and enemy in combat. He had fought a mountain lion and bear with nothing but a knife. He won both times and his rippling muscles had the scars to remind him of these battles for survival.

Kallah had been to the Eastern part of the Great Forrest. He saw another tribe that lived in a clearing there just three days walk from his tribe. He had been to the Western part of the Great Forrest where the hunting and fishing were good. But he had never ventured into it more than a week's journey into it. Every now and then, he would come upon the bones of someone from his tribe. Sometimes they were just collapsed in a pathway. Other times they were leaned up against a tree. Sometimes he recognized who it was by the remains of clothing nearby or still hanging about the bones.

Through the years Kallah had appeared before the Elders in the Tribal Council to ask them end the ritual of forcing tribe members to take a Walk with The Ancestors on their 60th birthday. Sometimes he asked for exceptions in the case of people he cared about. Other times he asked for an end to the practice completely. The Tribal Council listened politely but always gave the same response, No. One by one, Kallah watched his grandparents, mother, and father take the walk, never to be seen again.

In time, Kallah too reached his 60th birthday. The day before, he had appeared before the Elders in the Tribal Council to ask that an exception be made for him. He argued that he was still healthy and strong. The Tribal Council Members listened intently but once again said no. Kallah thought it was ironic that the Tribal Elders were all younger than he was. He knew he could kill any of them in a one to one battle but he could not kill his whole tribe. So the next morning, Kallah rose at dawn and began his Walk with The Ancestors.

Kallah walked for three days. He was tired but not too tired to continue. He stopped for a day. He killed a deer and ate well, and dried some of the meat over a camp fire. He put it in his nap sack. After two days he began to walk again. He walked past all of the places where he would go with hunting parties. He hunted and fished and ate well.

By the middle of the second week, Kallah was beyond where he went with hunting parties. He was in a part of the Great Forrest that he had never been to. He didn't know where the good hunting and fishing spots were. The dried deer meat he had made and kept in his knapsack sustained him during this time. He found a small clearing. The game was plentiful and a small stream supplied water. He stayed there for three months.

But then the game was less plentiful. The signs in the sky were telling him that winter was approaching. Kallah knew he wouldn't last the winter there. Kallah killed one last deer. He dried almost all of the meat. He dried the animal's skin and made a large pouch. He used its bone and sinew to sew the animal skin pouch shut. He made rope out of vines. He put all of the dried deer meat inside of the pouch. He decided he would walk to the end of the Great Forrest. He dragged the pouch filled with dried deer meat behind him to sustain him on his journey.

Kallah walked for three weeks. Then, one evening, he saw lights in the distance. The next morning he walked towards the place he had seen the lights. By midafternoon he came upon an encampment. There were 3,000 people living there. Many of the people were younger than him but a few were older. As he entered their camp, they looked at him strangely. Their language was different than his but he was able to communicate with them by making hand gestures and drawing pictures in the dirt. They told him they had never seen anyone from another tribe.

The tribe invited him to stay. After a couple of weeks he found that they knew less than the people from his tribe did. He ended up teaching them many new things. In time, they asked him to be their leader. As the years passed, the tribe grew strong under Kalah's leadership. Though he grew older, he didn't grow weaker. He was wise and still strong.

In his sixth year as leader Kallah noticed lights in the nighttime sky. There was smoke hanging in the air during the daytime. Then people began appearing out of the Great Forrest. They wore familiar clothing. They were from his old tribe. The first to appear were men in their twenties. They asked some of Kallah's tribe people to take them to the tribal leader. They took them to Kallah.

The men did not recognize Kallah. They asked to be allowed to be included in the tribe. They said that a fire in the part of the Great Forrest where they lived, had killed all but about 100 of their tribe. Kallah told them they could be included into his tribe if they followed the tribal rules. The men agreed.

As the people from the tribe began walking out of the Great Forrest, some of the older ones recognized Kallah. He was living proof that their ritual of sending their elderly out to die in the Walk with The Ancestors was a mistake. They took comfort knowing that they wouldn't have to take that walk in their new home.

Unique

VERSE 1
A man sees things in a different light
And has to fight for what he believes in
Is he wrong for not wanting to belong?
Or is the real wrong
The way that others treat him?
BRIDGE
Through ideas we change
And find a better way
If no one was willing to try something new
Where would we be today?
CHORUS
So is the man
Weird, strange, different
Or is he unique?
(repeat)
VERSE 2
A Sensuous woman becomes a liberated lady
And drives men crazy cause she won't settle down
Life holds more than kids and household chores
Now that her foot is in the door a career is what
she's found
(repeat chorus change man to lady)

The BobaBanana Saga

Gunderdink Parnoba was a 13 year old boy who lived in the capital city of the tiny nation of BobaBanana. BobaBanana is where most of the world's yellow, banana flavored Boba is produced for the global milk shake and smoothie market. The Boba business in BobaBanana was different than in most other places. The Banana Boba were not produced in large factories, they were made in people's homes. Because of this, everyone in Bobabanana made a decent living. Every one made just enough money to cover all of their bills, buy some new things and go on a vacation twice a year. Every family in BobaBanana was middle class. There were no rich families and no poor families. The people of BobaBanana had settled into happy, middle class lives.

Although BobaBanana was a small nation, its prosperity was noticed by the other nations surrounding BobaBanana. One of those nations, on the western border of BobaBanana was named Usetobesomething. Usedtobesomething was once as prosperous as BobaBanana. They made wonderful shoes out of Bird of Paradise leaves. They too had family run businesses making shoes. They too had a nation where everyone was neither rich, nor poor, but middle class.

Then, one day, about 20 years ago, Mr. Oldtimers Wiffenpoof a business tycoon from the nation of BigWiggia came to Usetobesomething and invested a lot of money in a couple of factories. He had an engineer design machines to make shoes. He took out radio ads offering good paying jobs at his Bird of Paradise Leaf Shoe Making Company factories. Many young people, wanting to break out on their own took the jobs. The jobs paid low wages but young people who lived at home liked the idea of having some extra spending money.

Within a few years, Usetobesomething changed. One by one, the family businesses closed down. More and more family members went to work in the Wiffenpoof Factories. Others, who were too old or too sick to work, weren't hired at the factories. For the first time in its history Usetobesomething had no middle class, just the working poor, the unemployed poor and the rich. The rich all had the same last name, Wiffenpoof.

One day, Oldtimer Wiffenpoof's son, Primo Wiffenpoof, wanted to make a name for himself. He wanted to establish his own tycoon status. All of the people who were able in Usedtobesomething worked for the Wiffenpoof Company. He saw an opportunity in neighboring BobaBanana. First, Primo sent agents in to buy up Boba Making Machines from families whose patriarchs wanted to retire. He paid huge sums of money for the machines and within a few weeks he was able to obtain 600 machines.

Next, Primo bought a gigantic piece of empty land near the Capital of BobaBanana. He built poorly constructed shacks using cheap materials and incompetent construction crews. The people of BobaBanana thought he was crazy, because no one in BobaBanana would trade one of their nice, middle-class homes for one of Primo's poorly built shacks.

Finally, Primo began building a factory. He continued buying up Boba making machines. It wasn't until the factory was actually built and the sign was put on that the people of BobaBanana knew what Primo was really up to. The sign read: "Wiffenpoof Primo Banana Boba Manufacturing Company". By this time Primo had acquired 6,000 Boba making machines, which represented 50% of all of the Boba making machines in BobaBanana.

The people of BobaBanana were upset but they took comfort in the fact that everyone in BobaBanana was either already employed or retired. Who could Crazy Primo get to work in his factory? Then, Primo imported 6,000 unemployed people from BobaBnana's other neighboring nation Gottagetajobnow. He gave them work in his factory and let them live in his poor quality shacks.

Within six months, the market for Banana Bobas was flooded. The Wiffenpoof marketing department took out ads which increased the demand for Banan Bobas. With increased demand and increased ability to make Banana Bobas, the Wiffenpoof Company increased its market share until, within a year, it controlled 75% of the market. The average household income in BobaBanana went down 75%. The only way BobaBanana could regain its market share was to out produce Primo's factory. The people of BobaBanana didn't know how to do this because there weren't enough Boba making machines. The entire nation became very depressed.

That's when 13 year old Gunderdink Parnuba remembered something. His Great Uncle, Gooptada Parnuba invented the Boba making machine. Once, when he was younger, he visited his Great Uncle. He was surprised to see thousands of Boba making machines in a warehouse he had on his property. When Gunderdink asked his Great Uncle why he had so many Boba making machines Gooptaba told him that he had made improvements in the machines but the original ones, while less efficient, never broke down, so many people still had the machines he made 30 years before.

Gunderdink sprang into action and called BobaBanana President Bootsy Cablehorn and told him about his Great Uncle's improved machines. The President became very excited. He and his advisors came up with a plan to obtain the machines from Gooptada Parnuba, give them to every family who retired and start the entire nation manufacturing Banana Bobas. In a radio announcement heard by the entire nation, President Cablehorn said.

"My fellow BobaBananians, we have acquired 8,000 improved Boba making machines and have given them to every family who wants to make Banana Bobas. This isn't a joke. This is serious business, the business of our nation and the very survival of our middle class economy. We'll regain our economy, and overtake the Wiffenpoof 's stranglehold on it. God Bless BobaBanana and all of our people."

The improved Boba making machines made three times as many Banana Bobas as the one's Primo Bought. They were also more efficient and made a better product. Within one year, the people of BobaBanana overtook Primno's company in both manufacturing and sales. They re-established their status as the world's premier manufacturer of Banana Bobas. President Cablehorn was re-elected and both Gunderdink and Gooptaba Parnuba were hailed as national heroes. Primo closed his factory and went home to his daddy, crying.

Dream Street

VERSE 1
On Dream Street
Every house is a mansion
The lawns are well kept
And the people dress in fashion
The nights are filled with passion

On Dream Street
There's a power everyone feels
Corporate executives

Making their big deals
The kind a handshake seals

CHORUS
On Dream Street
Today I am unknown
But one day
I'm going to make my home
On Dream Street
Life is like a fantasy
On Dream Street
I know there's a dream
Just waiting for me

VERSE 2
On Dream Street
They drive only luxury cars
You can go to a party
And mingle with the stars
Love never leaves scars

On Dream Street
The sun shines everyday
You can play at your work
Or work hard at your play
Your bills have already been paid
(Repeat Chorus)

Welcome To the Circus

Jane Greenway was dying. Everyone close to her knew it. She knew it as well. Her 5'8 170 pound body had been reduced to a 79 pound almost skeletal walking corpse by the cancer that racked it. Her once booming voice, was now faint and her condition frail. Her doctors told her that her body could not sustain life with less than 59 pounds. Jane was losing an average of 4 pounds a week. She knew she didn't have much time.

Jane's mother and three sisters took turns assisting Jane whenever they could. But all but one of them had full time jobs so they often congregated at her house during the early evening hours. Daisy and Susan were both younger than Jane and were trying to establish themselves in the corporate world, Daisy as an account executive at an investment firm and Susan as an associate at a law firm. Their mother, Evelyn, who didn't go back into the workforce until her daughters were out of college, managed a jewelry store. Only Julie, Jane's older sister, chose to be a homemaker instead of joining the workforce.

Jane's husband Bill owned a vending machine company. Jane obtained the money to fund it and she helped him run it. Since she got sick, Bill had to run both their business and their household. He had to coordinate which vending machines were to be restocked and when the refrigerator needed to be restocked. He had to decide when and who would pick up their son and daughter from elementary school as well as who would take Jane to her doctor's appointments. He did all of this on top of funding their household and Jane's mounting medical bills.

Bill had been struggling with Jane's cancer psychologically, for over a year. The stress he was constantly under took its toll. Never a very religious man, Bill had found religion a few months after Jane's diagnosis. He found a support system with the church's congregation and he found hope there too. He hoped with all of his heart that Jane would recover. He hoped that he would wake up and the past year and the disease that came with it would be nothing more than a bad dream. He still hoped for a miracle but his hope was fading. People from Bill's church came by often and held prayer vigils. They asked God for a miracle. They chanted "A miracle is going to happen for Jane." over and over for hours on end. Jane's mother and sisters didn't care for the new church. They were suspicious of the motives of the pastor and congregants who visited Jane. They secretly checked to see if anything of value was missing every time they saw "church" people at the house.

As hours turned into days and days into weeks, Jane wasted away as her family met and argued and fought over the disposition of her estate and where she would be buried. At first, they had the courtesy not to argue in front of her but as Jane got worse and she faded in and out of consciousness they acted as if she wasn't even there, although physically and sometimes mentally, she was right beside them.

Jane's mother and sisters wanted to have a big, expensive funeral and bury her in the family plot. Bill, who was still expecting a miracle refused to discuss such matters at first but as time went on, let Jane's family know that he wanted her to be buried in a plot adjoining his at a cemetery he had put down payment on two years ago. In keeping with the austerity of his new church, he wanted to have a simple ceremony presided over by the Church's Pastor.

Jane's mother and sisters tried to engage her in a conversation about where she would like to be buried, stressing their desire to bury her in the Family plot. Jane refused to talk about it. Her family mistook this as a sign that she was reduced to a semi-conscious state. Jane was conscious. She just didn't want to talk about her burial.

In her more lucid moments she wondered why her family was more worried about where she would be buried than what was to become of her children. She didn't worry though. She knew Bill would do a good job of raising them. She knew that reaching out to the church was his way of finding a support system to help him with the children. She knew that Bill never really got along with her family because they felt that he was beneath Jane. She also knew something her family didn't. Bill had the power to make all of the decisions regarding her funeral, burial and how he would raise their children and when and if he would "allow" them to visit with the children. She thought that her mother and sisters had better be nicer to Bill or he might just cut off contact between them and his children.

As she wandered in and out of consciousness, Jane tried to think about her life. She thought about her accomplishments. She thought about her regrets. Jane had only one regret. It was a boy named Johnny. Johnny was a boy from a town two states away. Jane met him at a dance when she was in her sophomore year in high school. They met at a dance but they never danced.

She saw him across the room and thought about how beautiful he was. A few minutes later, she went outside for some fresh air. Johnny approached her. They began talking. Johnny told her about his life and the big dreams he had. He was an artist and wanted to create beautiful things and in that way, make the world a better place. Jane told him about her dreams and he listened and was very supportive. They talked so long they didn't realize that the dance had finished. Johnny walked Jane home.

Jane really liked Johnny but she knew that her family wouldn't approve of him. A week later a letter addressed to Jane arrived. It was from Johnny. Jane and Johnny corresponded for the next two years. When it was time to apply for college she applied to a college about 50 miles from where Johnny lived. When it was one of the three colleges that accepted her, Jane told her mother that she preferred that college and told her why. Evelyn would not allow Jane to go to a college just to be near a guy. She reminded Jane that as Mother, she controlled the purse strings and she wasn't going to pay for an out of state college.

A few days later, while Jane was at school, Evelyn went through Jane's personal effects, found a bunch of letters from a boy named "Johnny", put them in an envelope and mailed them to the address on the correspondence. After a few weeks some letters from Johnny began to arrive. Evelyn just marked them "Return to Sender."

In time Jane noticed that her letters were missing. She confronted Evelyn, who told her that she had thrown them out weeks earlier. Jane tried to remember Johnny's address but like many things one takes for granted, she didn't realize how much she depended on the return address on Johnny's letters to write him back, until the letters were gone. She tried to reconstruct the address, sent a dozen letters to several of her reconstructed addresses but they all came back marked "No Such Number" or "No Such Address."

Three years passed. Jane attended a local college and forgot about Johnny. One day, a manila envelope arrived. It was from a woman named Evangelista. Evangelista wrote that she was Johnny's mother. She wrote to tell Jane that Johnny had been killed in an auto accident. She went on to tell her that her Johnny often spoke of Jane and wondered why she stopped writing him. She told Jane not to feel guilty though because Johnny found love with another, had a son and led a happy life until the day he died. She closed the letter by stating that her Johnny made a sketch of Jane from his memory of how she looked on the night they met. Jane turned the page and saw the sketch.

Jane treasured the sketch. She had it framed and hung it in her room. When she got married to Bill, she hung it in their room, directly across from her side of the bed. It hung there through the birth of her children. It hung there through all of their trials and tribulations of growing up, through recitals and science fairs and graduations.

It hung there 20 years later, when Jane was first diagnosed with cancer. It hung there during her many doctor's appointments and therapy sessions. It hung there still as she wasted away while her family argued over funeral plans. That sketch was the one tangible thing that connected her to Johnny and in the quagmire that was her life, it was the one comfort left to her.

Jane Greenway died quietly on a Sunday. Her family was engaged in an argument over funeral plans in the same room. No one noticed her taking her last breath or heard her utter her last word "Johnny."

No one except Jane saw Johnny, standing at the foot of her bed, wearing his letterman jacket from a high school two states away. Jane was beyond the heat of the raging argument and anger and animosities it raised. She was walking hand in hand with Johnny to a better place in another dimension.

Jane was buried on a Wednesday. It rained the entire time. Despite the weather and it being on a workday, 300 people attended her funeral. The members of the congregation wept openly as the pastor gave a speech about the good Lord calling Jane home because her work here was done. No one mentioned the fact that the miracle they had all prayed for never happened but some of them felt that way.

The battle over Jane Greenway's estate raged on long after her funeral. No one except the cemetery had noticed that Jane's family neglected to pay anything more than the down payment on her funeral and grave. The cemetery usually exhumed the bodies, whose families turned out to be deadbeats. They cremated them and re-sold the plot. But this didn't happen to Jane.

A few months after her funeral, a man who looked like a slightly older version of Johnny showed up at the cemetery and paid the balance of Jane Greenway's funeral and burial expenses with the credit card of a legendary movie star who was dying of complications from diabetes two states away. He was the movie star's personal assistant. He happened to read the Obituary of a woman whose name he saw on a love letter his father wrote that he just happened to find while rummaging through a chest that contained his father's personal affects, the night before. The obituary appeared in his local paper due to a clerical error on the form stating which towns the obituary was to run. It seems that the same conglomerate that owned the newspaper in Jane's city owned the newspaper in the town where the actor lived. This was one of many miracles involved with the final hours and death of Jane Greenway. They did still happen even if no one noticed them.

Dark Thoughts (Oh Mother)

VERSE 1
Oh mother sometimes I feel my life draining away
Ebbing away just like the tide
Oh father, sometimes I feel my life drifting away
Fading away into the cold black night
I have seen so many terrible things
Horrible things pass before my eyes
I long for the comfort a long sleep would bring
So come tuck me in and kiss me goodnight
For I am so weary and not thinking clearly
Truly frightened of the things that I might do
My dreams have been shattered
My soul left in tatters
I'm a shell of the man who you once knew
VERSE 2
Oh mother can't you see a little hope for me
Just within reach to keep me hanging on
Oh father I pray that you will give me the strength
To get through this pain and move beyond
Let the traumas I've been through all disappear
Like a nightmare so clear can vanish with the dawn
Leaving the ghost of my dark thoughts behind
Let me find peace of mind, so I can be strong
Let the light that's within me
Shine through this city

And illuminate every soul within its walls
Let a positive vision conquer superstition
And rise as a blessing to us all

The Mercy Date

Bob and Norm had been friends for many years. They had known each other since elementary school. They had gone through the tumultuous times of raging hormone disease in middle school together. Now in high school they both seemed comfortably settled in as students. Their social lives, however, were completely different.

Bob was smooth and confident in public settings. Bob was tall, thin, muscular and strikingly handsome. He had poise and charm. He liked talking to people and was genuinely interested in others. All of these qualities made him the kind of kid that girls were attracted to and other guys respected.

Norm was awkward in public settings. Like Bob, he was tall, thin and muscular but he wasn't strikingly handsome. He was very white and had a pasty complexion. He had blond hair that he kept in a perm. Originally from Brooklyn, he had a Brooklyn accent which might have made him attractive to some girls, if it weren't for his squeaky, high pitched voice.

Norm's biggest problem was his mouth. He said whatever he felt. He was brutally honest all of the time. His lack of ability to pick up on social cues and tact insured that he gave his brutally honest opinions and comments at the most inappropriate times. People might have forgiven his squeaky, high pitched voice and inappropriate utterances except for the fact that what made them was extremely disgusting. Norm's mouth was plagued with a gum disease which coated his gums with a yellow slime. Sometimes, when he spoke he would spray and people just didn't want to be sprayed with disgusting, yellow slime.

Bob knew Norm was well meaning. Like a true friend, he took Norm under his wing and schooled him on how to act in social situations. He helped Norm learn how to pick up on social cues. He had Norm work on controlling his vocal tone so that his high pitched voice was not so irritating. He taught Norm the art of tact. He taught Norm how to bite his tongue and refrain from speaking his mind. He taught Norm how to think it, without saying it.

Over the next few months, Norm was transformed into a well-spoken, "think before you talk" type of person. For the first time in his life, Norm was able to engage in social conversations with his peers. The new controlled Norm was able to make a few friends. He found that, because he showed respect to others, others began to show respect towards him.

Norm seemed happy but one day he told Bob that he was sad. When Bob asked Norm why he was sad, Norm told him that it was because he had never gone on a date. He told Bob that his friends were all going out on dates, yet he found himself sitting in his room, watching TV by himself on Saturday nights.

Bob wanted to help Norm. He knew that Norm had worked hard to transform himself into a more socially acceptable person. He knew that Norm deserved to be going out on a social date with a girl. Bob asked different girls that he knew if they would go out on a social outing with Norm. They all refused.

First, Bob asked them if they would go on a double date with him and Norm. Virtually all of the girls said no when they found out that they would be on the date with Norm instead of Bob. Then, he asked them if they would go out on a date with Norm alone. This time they all refused because of one thing, Norm's gum disease. All but one girl told Bob that they didn't want to be seen out in public with a guy who had disgusting yellow slime on his gums. The one girl who didn't tell Bob that, said that she couldn't trust being along with "that slime mouthed troll".

Bob had just about given up hope for Norm. Then, one day, Norm gave Bob a possible solution. He asked if Bob's sister, Lisa might consider going out on a date with him. Bob thought about it. Lisa had known Norm almost as long as Bob had. Bob told Lisa about the progress Norm was making and she seemed to be encouraging. Bob agreed to talk to his sister about the idea.

Bob's sister Lisa was tall, blonde and beautiful. She was one of the most popular girls in school. She didn't have a boyfriend but had gone out on social dates with a wide variety of guys. She had a good heart. If anyone would go out on a mercy date with Norm, it would be Lisa.

That night, Bob brought home a half gallon of Lisa's favorite ice cream. After dinner, he asked Lisa if she would go out on a social date with Norm. She said she would under certain conditions. First, Norm had to understand that it was a social date, not a romantic date. Second, that Lisa liked Norm as a person but was not interested in him romantically. Finally, the date would be just dinner and a movie, nothing more. Lisa told Bob that as long as Norm understood and abided by these three rules, she would go out with him that Saturday night.

Bob told Norm the next day. Norm was in heaven that whole week. He got his hair cut. He his car washed and detailed. He bought new clothes. Norm picked Lisa up at 7:00 P.M. sharp in his sparkling, clean, classic 1969 Chevy Impala. He walked Lisa from her door to the car. He opened the car door for her. He drove off with the Rod Stewart's song "Tonight's The Night" blasting on his stereo.

Four hours later Lisa returned rather upset. Bob asked her what had happened. Lisa told Bob that Norm took her to the movie theater and was a perfect gentleman. She said he took her to a nice restaurant for dinner and they had a pleasant conversation. It was when he took her home that something happened.

Lisa told Bob that when Norm got close to their house, he began to cruise very slowly. He eased into the parking space in front of their house. Then he puckered up and leaned in for a good night kiss.

"And..." Said Bob. "What did you do?"

"I ran out of the car and slammed that car door in his face!" She yelled. "I'm not going to kiss a guy with gum disease, what if it's catching?" She concluded.

Norm called Bob later that night. He couldn't figure out what had happened. He couldn't figure out why Bob's sister wouldn't give him a good night kiss. Bob told Norm it was because she made it clear that it wasn't a romantic date. Bob didn't have the heart to tell Norm the brutal truth. Norm never could figure out why Lisa never went on a second date with him.

Over the years, Bob and Norm drifted apart. Norm always carried a torch for Lisa. Bob's honest desire not to hurt his friend's feelings with the brutal truth caused Norm to have a lifelong scar and caused him to pine over a love that could have been but was never actually possible.

Powerless

BRIDGE
It was a struggle every day
Having to do what others say
It never went away
I was told when I'm older things will change

VERSE 1
When I was just a kid
What I was told was what I did
Then I went to school
Had to follow lots of rules

Couldn't skate out in the rain
Couldn't cry when I felt pain
I had no money, couldn't drive
How did I ever survive?

CHORUS
My life was just a mess
Cause I felt powerless

VERSE 2
Got a little older, got a job
When I got paid, I felt robbed
My paycheck couldn't buy

The things I needed in my life

I tried to improve myself
I got to vote but it didn't help
I called the bank to ask about a loan
They just laughed and hung up the phone
(Repeat Chorus)

VERSE 3
The wife and baby came along
For them I had to be strong
Got so many bills to pay
I'm desperate for an escape

Now it's like I'm in a cage
I have to act my age
Is the child in me dead?
I see him skating in my head

BRIDGE
It's a struggle every day
Having to do what others say
It never goes away
I'm told when I'm older things will change

(Repeat Chorus)

Safety First

Ace Johnson had been working for the Safety First Security Company for seven years. When he was hired, he was told that he would only be required to work from 9:00 am to 5:00 pm Monday through Friday. In all of his seven years with the company he held his employers to that limited commitment. He only worked 9-5 Monday through Friday. He never worked overtime and he never worked weekends.

Honoring his commitment to these hours and days was very important to Ace. He was never late and never absent. When he began working for Safety First, his wife was first diagnosed with cancer. Ace took the job because it was limited to those hours and it allowed him to spend time with his wife. Now, seven years later, she was still hanging on, but barely. He needed to spend as much time with her as possible.

Rudolf Biggy was Ace's boss. He started with Safety First the previous year. He had one mantra, "I will never work as anything lower than supervisor". In the year that Mr. Biggy was with the company, he never worked as a security guard, even in an emergency, he always found someone else to cover.

One Monday morning, Mr. Biggy approached Ace.

"Ace, he said, I know you never work evenings but I need someone to cover security at a Rap concert this Friday night."

"I can't do it boss," came a quick reply, "I need to take my wife into a new age clinic and Friday evening is the only time they have available."

"You'll have to reschedule," Mr. Biggy stated commandingly, "I need someone to work that concert and you are the only security guard available."

"The contract I signed with this company stated that I would only be required Monday through Friday 9am to 5pm, so you can't make me work any other hours." Ace replied.

Mr. Biggy's nostrils flared. "It's true, I can't fire you, but I can offer you a new contract, one with an extra $25.00 a week if you agree to work more flexible hours at the company's discretion".

Ace thought about the offer a minute. With his wife's medical expenses increasing, he could sure use the money. Then he realized that he could never buy back the time he didn't spend with her when she is gone. He decided to decline the offer.

A few weeks went by. Ace continued to work 9-5. Mr. Biggy treated Ace like crap. He gave him the worst assignments in the most violent, dangerous areas. Meanwhile, his wife got progressively worse. He muddled through the workday, rushed home to spend precious but ultimately sad hours with his darling wife and took her to a faraway, expensive clinic every Friday night.

One Monday morning, Mr. Biggy again approached Ace.

"Well Ace", he said with a swagger in his voice, "How do you like your new schedule?"

"I don't". Replied Ace abruptly.

"You know," Mr. Biggy continued, "All that can change. If you just agree to work a rap concert every Friday night I can switch you to the best work locations Monday through Thursday 9-5. Times are tough and I can't offer you any extra money but at least you'll have it easy the first four days of your work week."

"Didn't two other guards get injured working those Friday night concerts in the past few weeks?" Ace questioned.

"Sure Ace," replied Mr. Biggy, "But you could just as easily get injured any day of the week with the crap locations I've been sending you to."

Ace just ignored Mr. Biggy, clocked in and went to his work location for that day. The next day, Ace got a call from a neighbor. His wife was having convulsions. They called an ambulance. Ace left his work location and rushed to the hospital, just in time to see his wife for a few moments before she fell into a coma. She died later that day.

Ace called Mr. Biggy and told him the sad news. He told him he needed to take the next day, Wednesday, off to make funeral arrangements. Mr. Biggy seemed surprisingly understanding. Then Ace cried himself to sleep.

When he returned to work on Thursday, Mr. Biggy came up to him, put his hand on Ace's shoulder and told him he was sorry for his loss. Mr. Biggy gave Ace a very easy assignment that day. Ace was surprised by Mr. Biggy's new found compassion. He thought that perhaps Mr. Biggy wasn't the jerk Ace originally thought he was.

When Ace went back to Safety First to clock out that day, Mr. Biggy approached him.
"When is the funeral?" He asked caringly.

"Saturday morning", replied Ace.

Then Mr. Biggy asked, "So you can work the Rap concert this Friday night, right?"

A Silent Scream

VERSE 1
Deep in the crowd is a lady
Who is outwardly calm
But she's been touched
By injustice
She's felt and seen

And all of her feelings
Are crying to be let out
And build up into
A silent scream

CHORUS
There's a silent scream
There's a silent scream
There's a silent scream on the rise

There's a silent scream
There's a silent scream
Shattering the night

VERSE 2
In his hour of desire
A man is visited
By the cold and
Empty pain of

Loneliness

His weeping is voiceless
His expression says it all
As he clings to his
Pillow in bed
(Repeat Chorus)

A nation
Of people
Exploited and drained
By greed hunger
And power's thirst
Have all their frustrations
Channeled into a dam
Pretty soon that dam's
Going to burst
(Repeat Chorus)

How The Poems in this Volume are Related to the Stories.

Livin' On The Edge is related to everyone of the people in all of the stories in this book. It's about people who live on the margins of society and who don't feel positive effects of government trickle down economics. Yet, despite their lack of progress they hold on and wait for an improvement.

When Will We Communicate? is related to The Terror because the stranger in the store who spoke to the little boy was the first to actually communicate with him on a humanistic level. He treated the little boy like he was intelligent and reasoned with him using analogies that the boy could see as being truthful through firsthand observations in the moment.

Big City Girl is related to The Butterfly because she too is someone who gave up her dreams to raise children and is using what little time she has away from her children to enjoy the pleasures of a stranger's company before her looks faded and she found it impossible to attract a man.

Unique is related to The Old One because the main character in the old one has a unique perspective on the way his tribe treats the elderly and he uses that perspective to change not only the way he is treated but how the elderly are treated from then on.

Dream Street is related to The Boba Banana Saga as a satiristic counterpoint to the clash between two different economic views, the "everyone does okay" view of the islanders and the 1% view of the Antagonist of the story.

Dark Thoughts is related to Welcome To The Circus because it creates a visual landscape of dying with words. It represents the main character's feeling of dying and the desire to have her life mean something.

Powerless is related to The Mercy Date because the character of Norman believes he is powerless to change the way others see him. It is meant to illustrate how a feeling of powerlessness can follow one for one's entire life, no matter how successful one becomes.

A Silent Scream is related to Safety First because it represents the protagonist, Ace's anger and frustration at his life situation, coping with a dying wife and a crap head for a boss. At the same time it's a testament that others are going through similar feelings of anger and frustration.

Robot Chickens

The Great Bird Flu Super Pandemic began in 2037 when a disease control research facility accidentally broke 3 vales of the most virulent strain of bird flew and a worker vented the contents to protect workers in the facility that didn't have hazmat clothing available to them. A brisk wind carried the flu particles several miles past among other things, a poultry breeding ranch. The rancher had just loaded a truck full of 55 different breeds of chickens, ducks and geese to 23 different locations in 22 different nations on 6 continents.

The truck went to a small local airport. The poultry were then flown to Chicago Illinois and then to their various destinations via O'Hare International Airport. Half of all the poultry were destined for other poultry breeding ranches.

All of the poultry on the truck had breathed in the flu virus. They all were in the very beginning stages of the bird flu. They, in turn, infected the poultry at the breeding ranches they were sent to. Some of those birds were sent to other locations which had poultry and those poultry were infected as well.

It just took three weeks for the world community to realize that there was a bird flu pandemic affecting the world's poultry. Three weeks, however, was more than enough time for the pandemic to entrench itself into the domesticated poultry industry. Over the next few months, companies in that industry tried to save their livestock. When that didn't work, they sent people to raid feral species of poultry in their natural habitat. Within a year many of the natural species of poultry were compromised.

The second year found the poultry industry trying to breed poultry species in a sterile, germ free environment. Towards the end of the year, there was hope that the industry could be saved as several companies had successfully bred some species of poultry in sterile environments. Their hopes were dashed when the poultry couldn't survive outside of the sterile environment due to reinfection once they were removed or outside air got in.

Raising poultry in a sterile environment was prohibitively expensive and the industry could not afford to raise the enormous number of poultry needed to sustain consumer demand at restaurants and grocery stores. The industrial raising of poultry in a sterile environment was never meant to be more than a temporary solution. Industry heads believed that the pandemic would be cured in short order and they could resume with business as usual. As time and the pandemic rolled forward, poultry companies began to go bankrupt. Restaurants that featured poultry began to disappear. KFC became MIA. Churches Chicken became a cemetery. Popeye went down with the ship and El Polo Loco became El Restaurante Muerto. Poultry became scarce on supermarket shelves and on conventional restaurant menus.

The scarcity made a once common item with a cheap price tag more expensive to buy. Consumers worldwide craved poultry. In some cities, a single chicken breast sold for as much as $23.00. The poultry companies that were still in business sold off their existing stocks of poultry. One corporation even spent billions of dollars on an indoor, sterile, poultry raising facility one mile long and one mile wide. It contained everything from a hatching facility and incubators to a slaughterhouse, all indoors. It looked like the world would be safe for chicken lovers again. Unfortunately, the corporation located the facility in Kansas and a massive tornado tore it to bits along with all of its poultry.

Some unscrupulous companies began sold diseased birds. They knew that there was a danger in humans eating the diseased poultry but they didn't care. There were profits to be made. When consumers ate the diseased poultry, small numbers of them contracted the super strain of bird flu. The strain was beginning to jump species.

When the bird flu threatened to become a deadly pandemic amongst the human population, governments across the globe ordered the killing of all poultry within their borders. They ordered all businesses to destroy any poultry they had in stock. Keeping poultry as pets resulted in stiff prison sentences. Selling poultry on the black market resulted in the death penalty. Poultry were slaughtered in the wild. All of the slaughtered poultry were incinerated at 3,000 degrees Fahrenheit, the temperature required to kill the flu virus.

By the end of the third year of the pandemic, there wasn't a chicken, duck, goose or any other species of poultry in sight anywhere in the world. Chicken lover's pallets became cleansed of their favorite food source. Children's books and stories and songs about farms had to be re-written. Mother Goose was changed to Mama Piggy. Down pillows ceased manufacture and became prized family heirlooms.

After a few years, people had forgotten what poultry tasted like. Then, a wave of nostalgia over poultry swept over the world. Anything about any poultry that had been manufactured before poultry became extinct. Children's books about farms became instantly collectible. Memorabilia from chicken restaurants, recordings with songs about chickens, magnets, figurines and even coins, paper money and postage stamps that depicted any kind of poultry did as well.

All over the world people started reminiscing about chickens, ducks and geese. The Chicken Dance from the 1960's became a dance craze across the globe. Parents started telling their children about poultry. Donald Duck, Super Chicken became the most popular children's cartoons. The Cemetery where Colonel Harlan Sanders, Founder of KFC was buried became a popular tourist site and boasted over 600,000 visitors a year.

It was because of this poultry craze that Ulof Robotics decided to create robot chickens. The robots were about the same size as the original species they were imitating. Their hard wired aluminum body frames were fitted with synthetic "rubber" skin. Synthetic feathers were glued onto the skin, creating the look of a real chicken.

The look of a chicken was just the beginning. Ulof Robotics also programmed the robots to act like a chicken. Their robots walked like chickens. Given the ability to vocalize, the robots also made chicken noises, from calm clucking to loud cackling when danger popped its ugly face up.

The initial models went on sale in January 2041. They were priced at ^95.00 per unit. Their initial run of 10.000 robot chickens sold out within 3 hours! The company increased its second run to 50,000 units. It sold out in 8 hours. Within a month, Ulof Robotics had run 2 million units and there was still an insatiable demand for the robot chickens.

As the months passed, people all across the globe could be seen with robot chickens. Children played with them in their homes and slept with them in their beds. Adults walked down the street with them on a leash, like they used to when they walked their pet dogs. Robot chickens began popping up in TV commercials. A TV show starring a robot chicken named Chucky became immensely popular.

The plot of the Chucky Chicken show was that the chicken went around saving people. He led them out of burning buildings. He pecked away at muggers, bank robbers and salesmen. He flew up to tall buildings where people who were falling, being pushed off or jumping off of and brought people in danger to safety.

Ulof Robotics financed the show and used it to introduce the world to the next generation of Robot Chickens, ones that could think independently and act to help people. This new generation of Robot Chickens cost triple what the original generation did. People happily paid the price because of the popularity of the TV show. The new and improved Robot Chickens were flying off the shelves faster than the Ulof Robotics could make them.

Sales records of the new generation of Robot Chickens surpassed the sales of the original generation. The original generation was still selling at a brisk pace. By the one year anniversary of the release of the second generation of Robot Chickens sales had surpassed the 80 billion dollar mark. Stock shares Ulof Robotics became the most popular in the world, soaring to $6,000 a share.

Then the unthinkable happened. News reports out of Center City Iowa revealed that a 75 year old woman was pecked to death by a 2nd generation robot chicken. Within hours it went viral. Whether or not robot chickens were safe became the hot topic on news programs and blogs from Bangor Maine to Bangladesh. It took three weeks for the furor to die down.

A week after that, another death was reported. An 87 year old man in Nagoya Japan was electrocuted when a second generation robot chicken jumped into the bathtub with him. Press reports on the incident went viral. The Japanese Government launched an investigation. The key issue became whether the robot was trying to rescue the man who it may have thought was drowning or if it developed a defect that caused it to have a killer instinct.

Within one week, 15 other deaths were blamed on robot chickens. Nations across the globe began to ban the import of robot chickens. Lawsuits were filed, investigations were launched and remaining stocks of robot chickens were taken off of store shelves. "Killer Robot" Rallies sprung up across the globe. The rallies featured people throwing their powered down robot chickens in piles and setting them on fire with flame throwers. Reports began to surface about robot chickens escaping from their owners.

The next week began with Ulof Robotics filing for bankruptcy. The founder and CEO Olaf Ulof were arrested on charges of manslaughter in the deaths of customers the next day. Robot chicken began making solo, suicide attacks. A flight from London to New York crash landed at JFK Airport when a robot chicken flew into one of the jet engines as the airliner was approaching the airport. The resulting explosion ripped off one of the plane's wings. 385 people were killed.

The following week, a swarm of robot chickens swooped down and attacked people at a Killer Robot Rally. Some of the robot chickens jumped into the pile and began turning on the robot chickens in the pile. A gaggle of the robot chickens dove for the man who had the flame thrower. They began by pecking his arms and hands. Then they went for his eyes. The man with the flame thrower was pecked to death before he could fire it off. In the end 65 people were killed and 287 injured.

People were afraid to have Killer Robot Rallies after that. Instead they went on Killer Robot Hunting Party's. These featured large groups of people armed with guns of all types going out in search of robot chickens to kill. It was ironic because robot chickens were not living creatures. Many of the parties didn't result in the destruction of any robot chickens and some of them resulted in various pet animals or people accidentally being killed.

For the next month, robot chicken attacks became more frequent. Sometimes they attacked in packs or swarms. Other times they were solo acts. Robot chickens often hid in heavily populated areas, making military intervention impossible without high civilian casualties. It looked like the world would have to suffer the attacks for years to come.

When cross examined at his trial Olaf Ulof was asked when the robot chicken's batteries would run out. He replied that they would run out in 35 years. When asked if it was possible to stop the robot chickens, he stated that it was but that he wouldn't reveal how to stop them unless he was given global immunity from all criminal prosecution and lawsuits.

A global summit of world leaders met at the United Nations building in New York the next week. Ulof's proposal was considered. Some leaders were for giving Ulof immunity but many were against it. Some leaders from more totalitarian governments suggested their "agents' be allowed to torture Ulof and get the info out of him that way. In the end, the majority of world leaders voted to give Ulof global immunity, not because it was right, but because it was a better alternative than having to sustain attacks from robot chickens for the next couple of decades.

When Ulof was given the news of his immunity, he asked to be escorted to Ulof Robotics headquarters. When he arrived, he went directly to his office. He opened a locked drawer and flipped a toggle switch. Instantaneous explosions could be heard all over the globe. Ulof had a self-destruct chip embedded into every robot chicken in case he ever had to destroy them.

With the destruction of the robot chickens, Ulof's escorts left. Ulof caught a bus to the mansion in a nice neighborhood where he lived. He arrived to find his home boarded up with a sign on the front lawn. The sing read "Seized: Property of the U.S. Government." Later that day, Ulof found out that all of his bank accounts and other assets had met the same fate. He was immune from prosecution and lawsuits but he was penniless and had nothing left to win in a lawsuit. He had difficulty surviving as a hobo and died under a freeway overpass in Philadelphia six months later.

Sincerity
I've been stood up
Let down
 Passed over
And pushed around

Left longing
In bed
Misunderstood
Misled

I'm searching for a heart of gold
In a world of polyester alibis
I'm looking for someone to hold
Who won't leave me hanging on a string of lies

Sincerity
Every day
And every night
Sincerity
In all facets of my life
I desire
Sincerity

I've been
Run out
Held back
Steered off of

The right track

I've been taken
For a ride
Left mending
Broken pride

I'm searching for a heart of gold
In a world of polyester alibis
I'm looking for someone to hold
Who won't leave me hanging on a string of lies

Sincerity
Every day
And every night
Sincerity
In all facets of my life
I desire
Sincerity

Barter World

Halbert was dreaming. It was a sweet dream of a time in his youth. A time when people went into stores with shelves fully stocked, pulled out a piece of plastic, swiped it on a machine and walked off with so many bags of groceries they needed a cart with wheels to get them out to their cars. He awoke with a smile on his face.

Halbert stumbled to his kitchen and opened a drawer. He fumbled around until his fingers felt something he could trade. He pulled his hand out. A pen, perfect! He stumbled to his living room window. He opened it and looked two stories down to the crowded, dingy street below. Hal cleared his throat.

"I have a pen!" He yelled. "I'll trade it for a piece of fruit!"

"I have a banana!" Someone yelled from the crowd below.

"Let me see it." Asked Halbert.

A thin, middle aged woman with red hair, wearing a faded green dress held up a banana. Even from the second floor, Halbert could see that it was an over ripe, grayish brown.

"You've got to be kidding!" Halbert said. "I wouldn't feed that to a pig, assuming I could get my hands on one!"

Laughter erupted from the crowd. The woman with the banana blended into it and slinked away.

"How about an apple then?" A young man in his twenties in a battered, old, red, overcoat and black top hat said with a British accent.

"Let's see it." Asked Halbert.

The young man pitched it up to Halbert. Halbert caught it and looked it over. It was a large, red, apple. Not bad quality. Not bad condition. Hal decided he would be satisfied with the trade.

"Okay." Halbert said. "You've got a deal."

He threw the young man the pen. The young man tipped his hat to Halbert.

"Hey, what are you going to do with that?" Halbert asked the young man.

"I'm a writer. I'm going to write a story with it." The Young man replied.

"Well, when you have more fruit, call for Halbert. I have some paper to trade."

The Young man seemed happy and energized because upon hearing that, he put some pep in his step and walked away whistling a tune. It was seeing how happy that young man was at the prospect of having access to writing paper that made Halbert realize how fortunate he was. He was much better off than the average person. He had earned enough to own the apartment he lived in, on a floor above the throngs who lived on the streets, no less. Then again, he was one of the Barter Brothers.

Fifteen years before, a prolonged series of gigantic solar flares permanently disabled every satellite Earth had in the sky. Along with the satellites, the flares wiped out the internet and the global electronic banking system. In time, nothing electronic worked on the planet. All of humanity was reduced to bartering for the necessities of life.

That's when The Barter Brothers rose to local prominence. Halbert and his cousin Al were part of a group of people all over the globe, who were already engaged in bartering for things they needed. That group of people became the new entrepreneurs of the barter economy. They didn't make huge sums of money as entrepreneurs of past eras had but they were able to acquire literally anything they wanted.

At their zenith, about five years into the global barter economy, they were involved in many lucrative, multi-national barters of huge amounts of materials. Within a year after that, Bartering Corporations emerged and began taking over the global barter economy through mergers with, and acquisitions of, lots of small scale barterers. Halbert and Al merged with one the larger Barter Corporations about two years ago. They still made significant bartering deals but they got a much smaller percentage of the items that were being bartered. What's worse, for the most part, they had to take orders from corporate.

Halbert realized that he was late for an important meeting. Someone from corporate was coming down to their office to go over the Barter Brother's barters for the last quarter. There seemed to be some "discrepancies". "Discrepancies" were corporate way of squeezing barterers working for them for high value extravagant items left over from the barterer's share of profits from various barters.

Discrepancies were dangerous. They often meant having to make up for a shortfall of profit with suitable (meaning especially popular), barter items. If the "discrepancy" couldn't be satisfied with suitable bartered items in one's possession, it could mean losing a limb or body part because, those were the only things most people had, that were of any value. Body parts achieved such a high value status because a perfect match for someone who needed a body part would yield an extravagant barter to get it.

Halbert was able to obtain his apartment as a result of a barter for a kidney on behalf of the man who owned the apartment building. The man who possessed a kidney that was a match was reluctant to sign documentation to barter away his kidney but Halbert convinced him that he would get a small shed in someone's backyard for his family of four to live in. Halbert emphasized that the shed would guarantee he and his family shelter in the cold winter and hot summer months. The man who needed the kidney offered the apartment but Halbert had acquired the shed previously and he took the apartment without ever telling the man bartering away his kidney of its existence.

Halbert's partner Al, had to give up his left eye as a result of a "Discrepancy" several months back because the Barter Brothers didn't have sufficient suitable barter materials to satisfy that "discrepancy". Since then, Halbert and Al agreed to hold back a sizeable amount of the best merchandise from each barter so they could satisfy any "discrepancy" corporate might throw at them. They kept all of the best items in a warehouse behind their office so they could remit prompt payment for any shortfall.

Halbert exited his apartment, ran down the stairs and opened the big iron door that kept him safe. He emerged into the street. He saw a Pedi cab, a bicycle converted to seat a passenger. He called over to the driver.

"Hey, boy!" He shouted.

"Yes sir," replied a middle aged man whose skin was a mixture of deeply tanned brown and sunburn red.

"How much to go about three miles?" Halbert asked.

"What have you got to barter?" Replied the man.

"How about this." Halbert said as he pulled out a chocolate candy bar.

The man's eyes lit up. He stared at the chocolate bar and then at Halbert's face and then at Halbert's pocket, trying to figure out how many candy bars Halbert might have.

"Make it three chocolate bars and you've got a deal." He said.

"I've only got one other chocolate bar." Halbert replied. Then Halbert began walking away. "I'm sure I can find someone on this street who can give me a ride for two chocolate bars!" He yelled in conclusion.

"Are you sure you only have two chocolate bars?" The man said in a submissive tone.

"I'm sure." Said Halbert triumphantly.

"Okay, I'll take you." replied the man.

Halbert actually had six chocolate bars to barter for the ride but then, he was one of the Barter Brothers and how would it look if he allowed a lowly Pedi-cab driver to get the best of him in a barter?Halbert worked hard to disguise his delight at getting the best of that barter. The Pedi cab wound its way through the busy main street and then down a highway that went out into the suburbs.

About 35 minutes later, Halbert arrived at the office. As he entered he noticed that the man from Corporate was already there. The Corporate man's face looked irritated. Al had a frightened look on his face.

"Halbert, There's a problem." Said Al with a tinge of remorse in his voice.

"Why is there a problem?" Halbert replied

"I went over the shortfall and the items we have to satisfy it and..." Said Al.

"And what?" Asked Halbert.

"Nothing we have will satisfy the shortfall." Replied Al.

"Nothing? Asked Halbert incredulously. "Not even anything we have in the back room?" He continued.

"I'm afraid not." Said Al gloomily.

"What does corporate want?" Halbert asked with much trepidation.

"A body part." Replied Al grimly. "And guess what?" He asked.

"What?" Replied Hal.

"It's your turn." Al stated.

"Very well." Said Halbert.

Halbert hugged Al. Then he left with the man from corporate. After a short ride they came to a large clinic. Halbert knew that the law required people bartering their organs to sign legal documents authorizing the removal of their body part. Halbert and Al waived that legal right when they sold out to the corporation because they were not getting a bartered item in exchange for their body part, they were satisfying a debt.

They never knew what body part they were giving up to satisfy the shortfall. Al said, he didn't know he was going to be part of an eye transplant until he glanced at the chart on the door to the operating room. Halbert wanted to glance at the chart at the door to the operating room when he went in but he was given a shot in the arm when he was in the waiting room. After about an hour, he was loaded on a gurney. As the gurney rolled towards the operating rooms, Halbert tried to glance at the charts but his vision was too blurry. By the time the gurney entered the operating room and was locked down, he couldn't see at all. He could still hear though. The last thing he heard before he lost consciousness was:

"Is this the heart donor?"

Rat Race

VERSE 1
Can't get enjoyment
From collecting unemployment
You can't even hold your head up with pride
Your life is getting harder
You don't want to be a martyr
Though you think you might be dying inside
CHORUS
You've got to find a way to be free
From the heartless streets of a cold society
Your life's set at a cruel pace
You keep wondering how you got caught up into
this rat race
Wondering why you were born into this rat race
VERSE 2
Get an education
With a younger generation
To make up for the one missed in your youth
The pain is eased with liquor
But you're really getting sicker
Though you try to hide your face from the truth
(repeat chorus)
VERSE 3
The world keeps on turning
While your questions keep on burning

But you don't know where the answers will be
found
So you come to the conclusion
That there are no quick solutions
And confusion keeps your head spinning around
(repeat chorus, fade)

Mr. Boston's First Day

Mr. Boston woke up at 7:23 am. Realizing he woke up 23 minutes late. He sprung to his feet. Realizing that he had no time for a shower, he threw on the clothes he had picked out the night before and rushed out the door. It was strange that his alarm didn't go off. That was the first time in the eleven years since he first bought it, that it didn't go off. No worries, it was his first day, at a new school and he didn't want to be late.

Mr. Boston had been laid off from work for the past four months. He was laid off in mid-June and now approaching October, he was getting desperate to find work. Mr. Boston was laid off despite his seniority. This was probably due to the fact that his teaching credential was in Drama. The district had only six teaching positions for drama due to budget cuts that favored "Core Curriculum" classes. When the position opened up at Wingate, the new High School, he was one of eleven teachers applying for it.

He didn't recall hearing about Wingate before and wondered how a school district so strapped for funds was able to build a new high school but when an opportunity to go for an interview came up, Mr. Boston jumped at the chance to apply. He thought it was strange that Ms. Glee, the Principal at Wingate told him the school preferred a teacher with no wife and children, counter to most other schools he applied at. A job was a job however, and Mr. Boston had no time to ponder on such trifles, he had to get to work. Mr. Boston got into his car and sped the six blocks from his home to his new school.

When Mr. Boston arrived, the main office was empty. Suddenly, the door to the Principal's office opened and out stepped Ms. Glee.

She welcomed Mr. Boston to school and walked him to his class. She told him that children were rehearsing a play about a man abducted by aliens in his sleep. Then she left him to his students.

After observing them for about an hour and a half, he realized that the kids were talented and doing well. At 11:15 am Mrs. Glee returned to his classroom. She told Mr. Boston that he had to stay to rehearse with the students until 5:30 pm that night. Angered, Mr. Boston told her he would not stay and that he would file a complaint with the union because telling him to stay beyond his work hours without compensation violated the contract. Mrs. Glee replied that she couldn't afford any trouble with the union. She told him he could leave at his regular time, 3:00 P.M.

When the lunch bell rang, Mr. Boston wandered around until he found the school cafeteria. He selects his food and takes a plastic fork only to notice that it's full of grease. He tells the cafeteria worker this. She picks him up an even greasier one out of a bunch of plastic utensils floating in greasy dirty water in the sink. She hands it to Mr. Boston. He tells the cafeteria worker

"What is this?" Mr. Boston said.

"We wash and reuse all of our plastic utensils here. It's part of our efforts to recycle for a greener planet." The cafeteria worker replied

"The only thing green will be the skin tone of anyone using these filthy forks." He replied sarcastically. "These practices are against the Board of Health regulations I am going to have you all fired!" He continued as he stormed out of the room.

As he walked through the student cafeteria. He passes by many students eating and brushes aside students walking with their lunch trays. As he walked towards the exit door of the student cafeteria, he saw Mrs. Glee and the cafeteria worker staring at him from a window in the teacher cafeteria. He thinks it's strange and runs out of the exit door to the general campus.

Once outside, he decides to go back into the cafeteria and confront them. He goes back into the cafeteria and looks at the exact spot where they were looking at him only to find them gone. His heart began to beat rapidly. His head started spinning. He leaned on the wall of the main building for a moment. When the dizziness went away, Mr. Boston got into his car and raced home. He walked into the door. Everything looked normal. His furniture was where it was the night before. He entered the kitchen. It looked okay too. All of his appliances were there, but when he opened his fridge to get a beer, it was empty. He opened his cabinet to get some chips but it was also empty. Thinking he is going mad, he rushed to the bedroom to get his phone book. He opened his

nightstand drawer and found it empty. He picked

up the phone but got no dial tone. He went to the

bathroom to get an aspirin but the cabinet was

empty as well. He closed his medicine cabinet and

looked in the mirror. He saw Mrs. Glee and

cafeteria worked staring at him through the other

side of the glass. He threw a glass on the sink at the

mirror, shattering it. He ran out into the street

calling for help but nobody was there. He looked

into his neighbor's house and saw it was is empty.

He ran over to the next the next house on his block.

It was empty too! Then he ran into the next house

and another one after that. They were all empty! He

ran down the street peering into the windows of a

half a dozen more houses they were all empty!

Mr. Boston got down on his knees in the middle of the street and began crying. Mrs. Glee and the cafeteria worker appeared in front of him. Mrs. Glee began to talk to the cafeteria worker.

"Why is he crying? We did everything we could to make it easy for him?" She said

"I don't know," Replied the cafeteria worker. "Perhaps the space travel disrupted something in him." She continued.

"We tried so hard to make this look just like where he came from." Mrs. Glee said with disappointment.

"I know." Said the cafeteria worker reassuringly.

"Perhaps his memories were not downloaded completely." Mrs. Glee said.

"We'll have to try again tonight when he goes to sleep." Said the cafeteria worker.

"Let's reinforce the force field around this area, perhaps some of our atmosphere might have leaked in and affected him somehow." Said Mrs. Glee said as she began walking away from Mr. Boston.

"I sure hope not." Replied the cafeteria worker, following dutifully behind Mrs. Glee. "Our atmosphere would kill him for sure." She continued.

They walked away, leaving Mr. Boston Crying in the street. As they neared his home a couple of men in white overalls approached them.

"Make sure to fill up that object that holds cold stuff." Mrs. Glee told them. "And tell the others to reinforce the force field in this area." She said as they listened and then left hurriedly.

"Do you think he knows that he is going to live the rest of his life in our artificial "goldfish bowl"? The cafeteria worker asked Mrs. Glee.

"No, I think he will completely oblivious, at least for the first few weeks." Mrs. Glee replied.

"We can get plenty of time to observe and interact with him before then." Said the cafeteria worker.

"And so can the others who pay the fee to visit our interactive zoo." Said Mrs. Glee with a big smile.

Mr. Boston stayed in the street curled up in a fetal position, crying for several hours. He eventually cried himself to sleep. When he awoke it was dark. Walked towards his home slowly. As he got near to it he could see that the lights were on. He opened the door. All of his furniture was in the right place. He walked over to the kitchen. He opened the refrigerator. There was a can of cold beer and a couple of slices of peperoni pizza. He put the pizza in the microwave and turned on the T.V. An old movie called Blade Runner was playing. Within a few minutes the microwave beeped, signaling that the pizza had been cooked.

Mr. Boston sat on his couch, eating pizza, sipping on the beer, watching Blade Runner on T.V. He fell asleep. The next morning his alarm went off nine minutes late. He got out of his warm, cozy bed, remembering the dream he had. It was a nightmare. He dropped off his pajamas and got into the shower. He got his wash cloth, soaped it up and began scrubbing at as brisk pace. He knew that he was already running nine minutes late and he didn't want to be late for his first day at Wingate High School!

Escape

VERSE 1
Your way of life
Has got you down
People you meet
Are messing you around

PRE CHORUS
Got to get away
Got to get away
Got to get away
Got to get away

CHORUS
Escape
Got to get out from under this weight
Escape
Got to find a way to get your self straight

Escape
Your fortune is the chance that you take
Escape
Your future's in the move that you make

Escape
Escape

Escape

VERSE 2
The world has gotten
Too complex
From making ends meet
To having sex
(repeat pre chorus & chorus)

VERSE 3
Love and understanding
Is all you need
But you feel like a martyr
And you don't like to bleed
(repeat pre chorus & chorus, fade)

Precious Liquid

Hope was HIV Positive. She got the news when she went to the Red Cross to donate blood. She was devastated. Her emotions during the three months that followed the Doctor's pronouncement ranged from anger, to resignation. She even thought about committing suicide a couple of times.

She was gratefully relieved three months later, when a routine blood test revealed that she was no longer HIV positive. When she asked her family doctor how this was possible, he told her that the first test was likely a false positive. With that knowledge, Hope returned to the Red Cross to donate the pint of platelets she had promised to get credit towards her Senior Portfolio.

Hope was a thin but joyful 17 year old senior ad John Adams High. She had many acquaintances but few close friends. She was smart and kind and many of her peers at the school generally held a high opinion of her. Her parents were loving and supportive. They trusted her to make the right decisions and she rarely disappointed them. She spent most of her nights at home studying and many of her weekends at church or volunteering at the Senior Citizens Center.

On November 24, about five months after she first found out about the false positive HIV Test, she got a letter in the morning mail. The letter was from Medicorp Genetics. The letter stated that their staff came across her name when investigating the results of a trial being conducted on a new AIDS medication. The letter further stated that the company would pay her $250 for a brief interview and a blood sample at their headquarters in New York City.

Hope called the phone number listed on the letter and talked to a Mr. Merceless. She told him that she was interested in participating but was concerned about getting to the home office which was 200 miles from her home when she didn't have access to a car. He told her he would send a Limousine and asked when she would be available. She told him that since she was on vacation from school, she would be available anytime. He told her he was sending the Limo that day.

Hope told her parents what had happened and they agreed to let her go as long as she put the $250 towards her college fund. When the limo driver rang the doorbell Hope kissed her parents goodbye and told them she'd be back later that day.

The limo took 3 and 1/2 hours to arrive at the Medicorp headquarters in Lower Manhattan. Hope got so hungry she began eating one of the three candy bars she took with her. Hope was escorted to a conference room on the 26th floor. She was given an application to fill out. She filled it out in between bites of her remaining two chocolate bars.

Then, a couple of middle aged men in suits and a middle aged woman in a nurse's uniform came into the conference room. Hope shoved the remaining half candy bar and all of the wrappers into her coat pocket. The two men sat across the table from her and the nurse stood beside her. As the nurse rolled up the right sleeve of Hope's blouse to get a blood sample, one of the men began to interview her.

The man asked Hope questions about her general health. He then rattled off a long list of various diseases, none of which Hope ever had. Then he stated HIV. Hope froze. She told him that she had tested positive for it but that a few months later she was negative for it.

Then the other man, who identified himself as Mr. Merceless, told her that Medicorp staff thought that Hope might have something special in her blood platelets, something that might help with the treatment of HIV / AIDS. The men told Hope that the blood she donated to the Red Cross had been given to a patient that was part of their AIDS drug trial and that the man had improved despite the fact that he had received a placebo or sugar pill instead of their drug. They wanted the rights to do further testing on her blood to see if it might help any of other patients. They told her they wanted the rights to copy her blood or whatever was part of it that helped people.

Then Mr. Merceless put a long contract in front of Hope. He asked her to sign and date it. He told her that once she signed it, he would give her a check for $10,000 and a royalty for every shot, pill or vaccine they developed using her blood or its unique features that helped people. Hope was glad that something in her blood might actually help people. She signed the contract.

Hope was given a limo ride home. She clutched a packet which included the contract she signed, a check for $10,000 and $250 in cash. Her parents were ecstatic and told her that $10,000 would be a nice addition to the college fund which her parents began when she was born. It already had $35,000 in it.

As months passed, life went on for Hope. People from Medicorp would drop by her home every now and then to take some samples of her blood. The television news kept reporting on a new drug from Medicorp which cured AIDS. The Price of Medicorp stock skyrocketed by the time Hope received her first royalty check but it was only for a few hundred dollars.

Hope called Medicorp and asked for an explanation. Mr. Merceless explained that the drug containing the enzymes from her blood was very expensive and that only wealthy people could afford it. As a result, they were only selling about a thousand shots a month. He told her that they would, however, continue to pay her royalties and she could make a substantial sum of money over the next seven years, possibly numbering into the tens of thousands of dollars.

When Hope asked why the drug couldn't be given to more people Mr. Merceless explained that the cost of the research and development to create the drug had to be paid off before they could make the drug less expensively.

In early April, a news story broke reporting that Medicorp's research into curing AIDS came to a head when a patient in one of their trials got a direct intravenous infusion of the new drug and it cured his AIDS within days. The story stated that the new drug, which is injected directly into the blood stream, is nothing more than a synthetic type O blood the source of which is someone with immunity to HIV / AIDS. The story also stated that the drug cost about $200 per injection to make but that patients were being charged $100,000 per injection.

When Hope heard the news story, she became disillusioned. She called Mr. Merceless and asked him to lower the cost of the drug. She asked him to give it to everyone that was sick with HIV / AIDS not just those who could afford the $100,000 price. He told her to cash her royalty checks and shut up. Then Hope threatened to go to the press with her side of the story. Mr. Merceless quoted a section of the contract she signed. It was called a non-disclosure clause. It stated that she was prohibited from telling anyone about her arrangement with Medicorp, about her being the source of any drugs that use her unique enzymes a and anything having to do with the drug, or Medicorp.

Hope was dumbfounded. She felt angry and powerless. Then, she got an idea. She would volunteer at hospitals where there were AIDS patients and inject some of her blood into them. Hope went online and researched the correct way to give an injection with a syringe directly into the bloodstream.

Each week, she would volunteer at a different hospital. Each week she would inject as many HIV / AIDS patients as she could. By week three news stories began to break about entire wards of HIV / AIDS patients being cured. Soon afterwards, a man knocked on Hope's parent's door. He left a summons for Hope. Medicorp was suing her and her parents for $6,000,000 in lost revenue. There was another document attached called an injunction. It prohibited Hope from volunteering at or even visiting any more hospitals with HIV / AIDS patients.

Hope showed up for trial a month later. Her parents hired a lawyer but he was young and inexperienced. Medicorp laid out its case. It claimed that Hope had signed a contract. They had paid her royalties. A Clause in the contract prohibited her from selling, donating or otherwise giving away her blood as it was now proprietary property of Medicorp. Hope's lawyer tried to put up a defense but Medicorp's contract with Hope was Iron Clad. He even put Hope on the stand. She explained that it was wrong to sell the drug to the wealthy but the Judge told her that it may be wrong but it was not appropriate to the case which was about Medicorps exclusive rights to what is in her blood.

Just when it looked like all was lost and Hope and her parents would lose everything they had, the lawyer had an idea. He thumbed through the contract. Then he asked the judge to call Mr. Merceless to the stand.

"Now Mr. Merceless, are the dates on this contract correct and true?" asked Hope's lawyer.

"Yes they are." Replied Mr. Merceless after putting on his glasses and looking at the signature page of the contract Medicorp had with Hope.

"And Mr. Merceless, Hope's Lawyer continued, "Do the signatures on this page include all of the signatories for this agreement?"

Mr. Merceless looked at the signature page again. He saw Hope's signature, his signature and the signature of the Treasurer of Medicorp.

"Yes they are." He replied.

"And Mr. Merceless", Continued Hope's Lawyer, "To your knowledge, this is the only agreement between Medicorp and Hope?"

"Yes, it is the only agreement." Replied Mr. Merceless.

"How do you know that this is the only document between Hope and Medicorp?" Asked Hope's Lawyer.

"Because, as CEO of Medicorp I have to sign all documents of this nature and this is the ONLY document I have signed regarding our agreement with Hope and furthermore sir, if you or that young woman produce any other documents they are fraudulent." Mr. Merceless replied with a measured but angry tone in his voice.

Medicorp Attorneys had an opportunity to cross examine Mr. Merceless but they declined and Mr. Merceless was excused.

Then Hope's Lawyer called Hope to the witness stand.

"Hope" He asked, "Who do you live with?"

"My mom and dad." Replied Hope.

"And how old were you when you signed the contract with Medicorp?" He asked.

"Seventeen." Hope Replied.

As the words left her lips, there was a clamor among the Medicorp attorneys, they began rustling through some papers in files on their table.

"Your honor, I move that the contract between Hope and Medicorp be adjudged null and void because she was a minor living under the care of her parents at the time it was signed and therefore she didn't have the legal authority to enter into this agreement. Only her parents did and their signatures are nowhere on this document."

"We object your honor!" yelled one of the Medicorp Attorneys.

"On what grounds?" Asked the Judge. "We would like to enter into evidence this document, #R136, which we did deliver to the defendant's counsel in discovery." He said as he handed the Judge the document.

The judge looked it over. It was the form Hope had filled out when she donated her blood to the Red Cross. The same blood that was given to the patient in the Medicorp AIDS trial. The application listed a date of birth as November 23rd, which would make her 18 at the time she donated the blood. The Judge asked Hope to come up to the stand. Hope went into the witness box and was sworn in.

The Judge handed Hope the document and asked her if it was the true application she had filled out when she donated blood.

"Yes it is your Honor." Replied Hope "but..." she hesitated.

"But What?" Asked the Judge.

As she handed the document back to the Judge she said "You see that smudge over the first part of the month?"

"Yes." Replied the Judge.

"Smell it!" Hope stated emphatically.

"What?" Replied the Judge "Are you mocking me?" He continued.

"No Your Honor, it's just that that smudge is a chocolate stain that got on the paper because I was eating a candy bar when I filled it out."

The Judge smelled the paper.

"It does smell like chocolate." He said.

"The chocolate stain covered the DEC part of December so I guess the folks at Medicorp thought my birthday was in November and that's why they wanted me to sign the contract because they thought I was 18 but I wasn't and that's the God's honest truth!"

Just then Hope's Mother spoke. "Your Honor, may I approach the bench?" She said sheepishly.

"Who are you and what is your business with this court?" Replied the Judge.

"I am Hope's mother and I happen to have a copy of her birth certificate." She said.

"Approach the bench." Replied the Judge.

Hope's mother went to the judge and handed him Hope's birth certificate. The Judge read it over, cleared his throat and uttered:

"Medicorp's case is dismissed, the contract between Medicorp and Hope Langley is hereby declared null and void. All copies of the drug in Medicorp's possession shall be destroyed and Hope, now being 18, will be free to contract with any party she wishes."

There was a media frenzy over the case. Medicorp destroyed the drug as ordered. Hope became an overnight celebrity. Scores of drug companies offered her huge sums of money to manufacture the drug but Medicorp appealed the ruling and got an injunction against Hope contracting with any other parties. Everyday hundreds of people were lined up outside of Hope's parent's house, begging her to give them an injection of her precious liquid.

With her hands tied and her desire to help sick people, Hope had no choice but to begin giving people who came to her door injections. She could only do this once every two weeks and AIDS patients sent her thousands of letters asking to be chosen for an injection.

Every two weeks, Hope's mother called the patients selected. They appeared at the sidewalk in front of Hope's home. When her father opened the gate, they walked up the walkway and she gave a life saving them an injection. In between the times when Hope could give blood, she was reading letters from dying people who wanted to live. She carefully selected as many as she could. She hated playing god and wished she could select everyone but she had a limited amount of blood to serve an unlimited number of people who needed it.

Five months after Hope began giving out her blood, she awoke on a transfusion day. She drained the precious liquid from her veins and put it in a plastic bowl, which she ten used to withdraw portions with a set of a few dozen syringes.

Hope had just loaded a small cart with syringes full of her blood. As she walked out from her house a middle aged woman emerged from the crowd and shot Hope three times in the chest. Hope fell onto the cart which collapsed under her. All of the syringes fell off and broke. By the time Hope reached the ground, she was dead. The Crowd stood motionless in surreal disbelief.

"That bitch killed my son" Shouted the woman who shot Hope. "He was about to get an injection from Medicorp when she won her trial. He never got it and he died today!" She concluded.

Then the crowd suddenly went wild and savagely tore the woman limb from limb, pouncing on the pieces of her bloody body parts. The cure for AIDS would not be found until the next decade.

Lost Between Two Worlds

VERSE 1
I'm confused
And I feel like I'm being used
I may be young
But I've been aged by all that I've been through
BRIDGE
Cause I've been shut in
Between the old and the new
Shut out
With no one to turned to
Turned on
To the wrong kind of high
Turned into
Society's fall guy
CHORUS
I'm lost between two worlds
One lies dying
The other crying to be born
Lost between two worlds
Paradise's promise
And hell fire's scorn
VERSE 2
Reality
Is wrapped within a fantasy
I'm young and broke

Dreams are all that I can get for free
(repeat bridge & chorus)

The Juice Fly

The service was slow at the restaurant. It was a large place with a small wait staff and a lot of customers. The Branfield family hadn't seen a waiter in at least ten minutes. Becky, the mother of the family was hoping to get her glass of watermelon juice re-filled but since she hadn't seen a waiter in a while she decided to drink the 10% of the juice she had been saving for one last refreshing swallow before it was re-filled.

She put her hand around the glass and before lifting it to her mouth, looked down at the wonderful tasting juice. She was shocked to see a large, ugly fly crawling on the inside of her glass! Becky picked up the glass and swirled the juice around, the thick, swirling liquid caught the fly by surprise and it was swept into the juice.

"Oh baby, you're cruel." Said Jack, the father of the Branfield family.

"Serves the damn thing right!" Said Becky "For having the audacity to invade my precious last swallow of juice." She continued.

As the family sat there waiting, Jack couldn't help but notice the fly in the glass of juice. It was swimming in the juice. Becky thought she had killed it but all she managed to do was immerse it in juice in the center of her glass. The fly kept on swimming to the point where the juice touched the side of the glass, once there, it would move its legs quickly to try and lift itself out of the juice and onto the side of the glass, then try to grab onto the side of the glass, lift itself up and climb out of the glass to freedom. It was unsuccessful, however, because the juice that coated its legs denied it the friction it needed to climb out of the sea of juice. After a few seconds, it would tire, stop swimming and float to the middle of the juice where it would begin the process again.

The fly kept on doing this, over and over again, for five minutes. The Branfield children Emma and Graciela noticed their father watching the fly in the juice and soon, they began watching the fly as well. Jack overheard the girls call it the juice fly. Jack was moved by the fly. Becky thought that she had killed it but it didn't know it was supposed to be dead. The juice fly was in an impossible situation. It would never get the traction it needed to lift its body from the thick liquid it was trapped in. It would never gain its freedom. Yet it continued to try over and over again.

"Are you going to look at that stupid fly all evening?" Becky told Jack, breaking his concentration.

"No." Replied Jack, momentarily looking away from the life and death drama played out in a glass of juice.

Jack looked back at the glass. It was gone!.
Emma had taken it and was blowing in the glass.
Every time the fly swam towards the edge of the
glass, Emma blew it back to the center. Then
Graciela joined Emma and they both blew the fly
all over the circumference of the glass, all the while
yelling "Juice fly. Juice fly, when will you die?"
Then Emma dropped an olive into the glass of juice
in an attempt for it to land on top of the fly to
drown it once and for all but she missed horribly.

Then Jack grabbed the glass. He brought it
towards him, stuck his finger into the thick liquid.
He brought the fly to the top of the glass and said;
"Your hard work shall be rewarded little fella!"
Then, he cupped his hand put the finger with the fly
into it and walked out of the restaurant.

By the time Jack exited the restaurant, he saw that the fly was beginning to move inside of his cupped hand. Jack set the fly to rest on the leaf of a nearby tree. He went back into the restaurant washroom and washed his hands. Then he returned to his families table. Just as he sat down, Becky spoke to him.

"That was disgusting!" She said. "Sticking your finger into my glass and pulling out that dirty fly." She continued.

"No, what's disgusting is teaching our daughters to kill living creatures." He replied angrily.

"I didn't tell them to do it." Replied Becky.

"No, you didn't." Jack said. ""But your silence spoke volumes." He continued.

"What's a stupid fly ever going to do for you?" Becky asked.

"It's not about what the fly can do for me, It's just a dumb fly but it wanted to live. Once seeing that, that will to live, why would you kill it? Replied Jack. "Besides, there is such a thing as Karma." He continued.

"Karma?" Becky questioned incredulously.

"Yes, Karma. That fly couldn't help that he was born a fly. You do cruel things to a fly and in turn, sometime during your life, someone does something cruel to you." He replied.

Then a waiter finally showed up. Becky complained about the fly in her juice so the restaurant comped the cost of the Branfield's drinks. They ordered desert. It came promptly. They ate it without saying a word, paid and left the restaurant.

As they left the restaurant, Jack looked at his watch. It was after 10:00 P.M. The large parking lot, which had been filled when they arrived at 8:15 P.M. was almost completely empty. Since the lot was full when they arrived, they parked in an unlit section at the far end of the lot. As they got close to their car, a figure emerged from the shadows. It stood directly in front of Jack.

"Give me your wallet!" The figure demanded. Jack, who was an amateur boxer ten years before, when he was in his late teens and early twenties, knew he could likely deck the guy with one punch. He didn't know what kind of weapon the guy had and he didn't want to risk hitting the man directly because there was a danger he might have a gun and end up firing his weapon when punched, putting Becky and the girls in danger. If the figure however, it might give Jack the opportunity he needed. Jack hesitated.

"Give me your wallet!" The man demanded again.

Suddenly, Jack heard a buzzing noise. The figure heard it too. The buzzing moved towards the figure. The man began swinging the hand without the weapon over his head, in an attempt to swat at whatever was buzzing. The buzzing persisted and the man kept swatting. One of those times, the moonlight illuminated the man's hand and Jack could see that he was not holding a gun or even a weapon, but an inhaler covered with what appeared to be shoe polish. Jack knew that the man was no real threat. The next time the man swatted at the fly, Jack took a swung at him, giving him an uppercut just below his chin. The man fell backwards, hitting the ground unconscious. The moonlight lit up his face. A fly landed on it, its wings had a watermelon colored tint to them.

Becky whipped out her cell phone and dialed 911. She told the operator what had happened and where they were. The operator told her that a police car would arrive within two minutes.

"You don't suppose that was the same fly you rescued do you?" Becky asked.

"Karma baby." Jack replied.

"Karma?" Becky replied.

"Actually in this case…" Jack began. "Instant Karma." He concluded.

EVERYDAY HEROES

VERSE 1
Blue collar man commuting
Wants to get to work on time
He works in a factory
On a long assembly line
Next to him sits a clerk
Who's thinking about asking for a raise
All day he works shuffling papers
But without much praise

CHORUS
Everyday heroes
Are the world's helping hands
Everyday heroes
Are the heartbeat of this land

VERSE 2
An aging secretary
Types the hours away
She doesn't mind hard work
As long as she gets equal pay
A housewife turned cashier
Stands o n her feet all afternoon
The customers aren't always friendly
Yet she smiles her whole shift through
(repeat chorus)

VERSE 3
A young cowhand brands a steer
And looks up towards the setting sun
Its not the loses that he thinks of
But the small victories he's won
A farmer ends his day of toil
Heads for home and puts away his plow
As he walks in the door for dinner
He wipes the sweat off of his brow
(repeat chorus, fade)

Her Rash

When he arrived at her apartment and knocked on the door he didn't know what to expect. Richard had joined the blind dating service out of desperation. He was a busy executive with little time to go places to meet women. The service sent him an email with Alma's phone number on it. They chatted a couple of times before she agreed to go out with him. Now, as he stood in front of her door her closing words in their last phone conversation echoed in his mind.

"My roommates told me I should go out more often so I guess I'll go out with you." She said.

The door opened and a petite, rather beautiful woman was on the other end of it.

"Are you Alma?" Richard asked hopefully.

"Yes", she replied. "You are Richard, right?"

"I sure am." He responded.

With that she followed him to his shiny, new sports car. He opened the door on the passenger side and she got in. he began driving. Alma was different from the other girls he met from the dating service. She was actually attractive to him but he wasn't sure if he was attractive to her. He sensed a slight sense of disappointment in her eyes when she first opened the door and saw his tall, gangly appearance.

The car sped down the surface streets. When Alma asked where they were going to go Richard told her that they would be going to the upscale Westgate neighborhood where he lived even though it was 20 miles from her house. After a few minutes they entered the freeway. Within a few moments they were stuck in bumper to bumper traffic. Richard realized that a trip of less than a half an hour would now grind down into an hour and a half. He tried to break up the monotony of sitting in traffic by conversing with Alma but she was just responding with one word answers to his questions.

Somewhere in the middle of his questions he noticed that Alma began to scratch her arm. Just slightly at first but as time pressed on, her scratching became more vigorous. He wanted to be polite but he was curious as to why such a beautiful young woman was scratching her arm almost non-stop.

"Why are you scratching your arm so much?" Richard asked with concern.

"My rash, its coming." Alma replied.

As the car weaved its way through traffic, Alma kept scratching herself. The closer they got to Westgate, the more ferocious her scratching became. Finally, two hours later, he pulled into a parking lot. Richard got out of the car and opened the door on the passenger side. As Alma got out, he noticed that she was covered in dark red blotches.

"Oh my God!" Richard exclaimed, "What happened to you?"

"My rash, it's here." She replied.

"Do you want to stop by the pharmacy and get some lotion or something?"   Richard said with concern in his voice.

"No," Alma replied. "I think I'd rather just be driven home now." She continued.

With that, Richard got back in the car, drove back onto the freeway and slowly weaved his way back towards Alma's neighborhood. They didn't exchange a word during the ninety minute return trip. When they arrived at her apartment building Alma got out of Richard's car and ran into apartment.

Richard never called her again. He wondered if her rash was something that she had recently come down with, a recurring problem or merely an allergic reaction to him. Then he wondered if she somehow knew that he had raped the five women from the service he had previously dated. He wondered if she was psychic and knew he was planning on raping her too.

He thought he should pull over and think this out in case he had to go back to her house and take care of her. While he was thinking this, he ran a red light and an eighteen wheeler plowed into his nice car. It was hard for the coroner to figure out just what was going through Richard's mind at the time of the accident because what the weight of the truck didn't crush, the heat of the fire that engulfed his car when his gas tank exploded consumed. What was left of Richard couldn't fit into a box of Kleenex.

Get Me Through The Night

VERSE 1
No the pain ain't gone
But like the taste of a bad cigarette
It lingers on

I've been taken for a ride
And now I'm slowly but surely
Dying inside

BRIDGE
You've always been there
When I've needed you before
And right now I'm hoping
That you will be there for me once more

CHORUS
Get me through the night
I'm so cold and lonely
Don't want this emptiness to own me

Get me through the night
Cause I'm losing my grip
And I'm counting on your friendship
To get me through the night

VERSE 2
Well, I'm trying my best
But I seem so far away from
Happiness

This thing is dragging me down
Now's the time I need a friend
Like you around

(repeat Bridge, Chorus, hook and fade)
You can hear this song by googling bandcamp and once on bandcamp, typing in the loveforce collective.

The Highway Fire

I was on my way home from work one weekday afternoon. A brush fire on the highway forced a lot of cars to flee to the nearby surface streets. I went to a main thoroughfare that led within a mile of my home. That thoroughfare, however, was not made to accommodate such a large number of cars.

I had been in bumper of bumper traffic for over 90 minutes and had only gone two of the five miles needed to get home. It was 96 degrees that day but between the heat generated by the nearby brush fire and the bumper to bumper cars, the air temperature where I was, was a whopping 122 degrees. I knew I should have fixed my car's air conditioning but I would have had to replace the compressor and I couldn't afford the $800 it would have cost to do that. So, there I sat, in my hot car, with all of my windows down, stuck in traffic with 122 degrees of heat producing beads of sweat the size of bullets all over my entire body. I was soaked in my own sweat and upset at the entire situation.

Then, suddenly, the traffic stopped moving forward. It took me 40 minutes to figure that out because we had been moving so slowly before, it took a long period of time to determine that the movement had stopped altogether. As each minute of killed forward motion ticked away, I began to get more and more irritated. I wondered if would die of heat stroke. That idea wasn't too farfetched considering what I had been through. Something eerie was going on all week. It was, as if, the Grim Reaper himself had been stalking me.

On Monday, a big rig jackknifed right in front of me. If I hadn't slammed on my brakes, at the exact time I did, its payload would have crushed my car like a gorilla can crush a can of soda. On Tuesday, I was about to get on the elevator on the 62nd floor when my wife called and, knowing I could not get reception in the elevator, decided against getting in. The cable on that elevator snapped and it plunged 62 stores hitting the ground floor at 110 miles per hour. Everyone on it died. On Wednesday, a steel beam from a construction site at a neighboring building got loose and fell 13 stories crashing through my office window. Fortunately, I was in the bathroom answering natures call at the time. Yesterday, Thursday, I almost went to lunch with some of the people from the office and they all got food poisoning. One person was even hospitalized. She died of an allergic reaction to whatever was in the food. That could have been me. Tonight, I just wanted to get home so that the relaxation of the weekend could just wash away the stench of death that had been around me all week long.

The guy I the car next to me turned off his engine. I decided to turn off my engine too. A lot of the cars nearby did the same. "That should cut down the heat a couple of degrees" I thought to myself. People began getting out of their cars. I did too.

I looked forward. I could see about a half a mile down the road. Everything was stopped. Nothing even had a prayer of moving. I looked behind me. No one was going anywhere there either. I even looked on my left side to a dirt road on a hill beside the thoroughfare I was on. Even traffic there was stuck!

Then, I noticed smoke coming from the other side of the hill where the dirt road was. Could it be that the highway fire had burned its way to where I was? Within minutes I saw the unmistakable yellow orange glow near the crest of the hill which told me that the fire was about to breach the ridge and come down the other side where the cars on the dirt road were stuck in bumper to bumper traffic.

The cars on the dirt road tried to move. Some went forward. Some went into reverse. None of them got very far. Suddenly, a flatbed truck came barreling down the hill, just ahead of the flames. Cars on the dirt road maneuvered to give the truck some space to either drive past them or pull in amongst them. I could see panic on the flatbed driver's face.

As the truck neared the dirt road, the driver slammed on his brakes. He entered the space the other cars made for him and made a sharp turn with the brakes applied hard the whole time. The truck ended up in the line of cars but with the driver's side teetering on the edge of the road with a five story drop beneath him.

Something in the back of the flat bed was on fire! The driver moved over to the passenger side of the cab and got out. Then I saw him on the back of the truck flailing his coat trying to smother the flames. He was oblivious to the fact that the fire was making its way down the hill towards the dirt road the cars were on. Drivers began to exit their cars, looking up at the flames slowly moving towards them.

Then, out of nowhere, a fire Department plane swooped in and dropped what must have been a cubic ton of water on the crest of the hill at the top of theslope directly over the dirt road the drivers were stuck on. Water cascaded down the slope, dousing the flames. Drivers scrambled into their cars just as the beginnings of the flood of water were about to reach them. The water had enough force to sweep someone off their feet but not enough to move a two ton vehicle sideways off a cliff.

The flatbed, which was already teetering near the edge of the road shifted slightly as the initial crest of the water drop reached its tires. The driver noticed and jumped off the truck immediately. It was then that I noticed the truck was almost directly above my position on the road. I eyeballed its trajectory should it fall and realized that it would land on my car. I began running forward as fast as I could.

Within moments I could hear the crash bang sound of the flatbed rolling over as it plummeted down the hill. I heard it crash onto the street below, crushing cars beneath it. I heard an explosion. I felt its force knock me down. I was stunned but got up. I had enough of close calls. I just wanted to get home. I began running. I didn't look back at my car, but something told me it was totaled. The heat of the day, the nearby fire, the idling cars really got to me for a moment and I stumbled and fell again just as I reached the intersection about a half a block from where my car was. Then, I got up and with new found energy, I began running towards home as fast as my feet could carry me.

I ran a few blocks. Surprisingly I wasn't tired. Perhaps I was experiencing an adrenalin rush triggered by fear or anger or frustration I had been feeling. I ran past restaurants, a mall, and my bank. When I got about a mile down the road I saw a traffic accident that must have caused all of the backup and stagnation in the traffic. After another mile I reached the intersection of the thoroughfare I was driving on and the highway that led to the street I lived on. Several police cars blocked the road. There was a sign that said "Emergency Vehicles Only".

I picked up my pace, knowing that I was only about a mile from my house. After a couple of blocks I noticed that there were no cars at all. I decided to run right up the middle of the lonely highway. Lost in my thoughts, I barely noticed a blue ambulance speeding down the highway in the opposite direction. I jumped out of the way just as it passed me. It was another close call in a week of too many close calls. I continued down the highway undaunted.

When I got to my street, it struck me how exactly, as I left it that morning, it was. There were obviously no fires here. I made my way to my house. My two dogs were looking out the big bay window in the front of the house. They were barking away. I realized that I had left my keys in the car. I was going to try and break into the house when I realized that I didn't see my wife's car. Where could she be? I began to worry about her safety.

Then I heard her voice. It was calling my name. "I'm here dear!" I replied but she didn't seem to hear me and I couldn't see where she was. I wished I could see her.

Suddenly, I felt something pulling me backwards. It was a strong force I had never felt before. It was like an unseen hand had grabbed me from behind and was dragging me somewhere. It transported me backwards. At high speed, I went back down the lonely highway that led to my home, back past the Emergency Vehicles Only sign and up the thoroughfare where I was stuck in traffic, past the accident that caused the backup and my bank and the mall and the restaurant to the intersection where it all began.

I saw my wife standing on the outskirts of a large crowd. She was calling my name. I began calling back to her. "I'm here baby!" I'm right here!" She walked into the crowd and disappeared. I kept on calling for her but the density of all the bodies in the crowd must have drowned out my voice.

I walked into the crowd. Everyone had their backs to me. They were all looking at something ahead of them but I couldn't see what it was. I pushed deeper into the crowd. Then I saw my wife. She was exiting the crowd and walking into the intersection. As I got closer I could see she was sobbing. Then, I saw what she was looking at.

In the middle of the intersection was the blue ambulance that had passed me on the lonely highway. In front of the ambulance was a collapsed heap of a person, badly burnt cradled in the arms of an old woman. The old woman looked a bit like my dearly departed mother. Wait a minute, could it be? It was my mother!

A paramedic walked up to my wife and put his hand on her shoulder to comfort her.

"A flaming truck rolled down that hill and crushed your husband's car." The paramedic said. "He escaped that but an explosion from the impact of that truck with your husband's car set him on fire. He got up and began running but it wasn't long before the flames took him down."

"He was just trying to get home…" My wife mumbled in reply, as if in a trance.

Then my mother got up and walked over to me as the other paramedic put a sheet over my body.

"Come child, there's nothing more for you here. I have been trying to bring you home all week."

FREEDOM

VERSE 1
I've been down
So very long
Imprisoned in
My life's situation
Hungerin' for some kind of escape
Eager in
My anticipation

PRE CHORUS
But now
I've finally
Discovered
A way out
And if you
Come looking for me
I can be
Easily found

CHORUS
In my freedom
Oh, yay, yay
From the economic chains that bind me
Freedom
Going to leave all my problems behind me

In my freedom
Be the kind of person I want to be
In my freedom
Lead the kind of life I want to lead
In my freedom
Freedom
Freedom

VERSE 2
It's tough
Being out there
All by myself
To face the competition
Wonderin'
What tomorrow will bring
Solid in
My personal ambition
(repeat pre chorus and chorus, fade)

How The Poems in This Book are related to the Stories

Sincerity is paired with Robot Chickens as a counterpoint to the fact that all of the authentic or sincere chickens in the world have died off and now all people have is fake , insincere robot chickens to take their place. As humankind continues to pollute and desecrate the world, species will continue top die off and we will be left with robot replicas to remind us of the real animal that once lived.

Rat Race is related to Barter World because it symbolizes that even in a world where barter is the basis of the economy, humankind will still be enveloped in a rat race. We shall still have to struggle to earn our daily bread no matter what our economy is based on.

Escape is paired with Mr. Boston's First Day because Mr. Boston is stuck in a time loop. He doesn't seem to know this but he secretly would like to escape and in a way, the time loop he is stuck in provides an escape every night when he goes to sleep.

Lost Between Two Worlds is related to Precious Liquid because the protagonist of that story is lost between two worlds in several different ways. First, she is a teen struggling between childhood and adulthood. Second, at the beginning of the story she struggles with facing her mortality because she thinks she has a deadly, incurable disease and then she finds out that she is immune to it and indeed, is the cure for it. Third, she is caught between her desire to control the way her blood is used because her desire to make her blood affordable is in direct conflict with the corporation's desire to profit from it.

Everyday Heroes is related to The Juice Fly in a complimentary fashion. The story illustrates how a lowly fly can become a hero and the song illustrates common people who are not always thought of as heroes but who are, none the less the real heroes of life because they show up and give 100% day after day and year after year.

Get Me ThroughThe Night is related to Her Rash because the protagonist, the girl on the date somehow knows that she is in danger and needs to get through the night just like the character in the song needs to get through the night. Further, the night in both the story and the song are symbolic for the hard times we all go through at various points in our lives and a testament to the very human ability to ride through the storms of life and come out better on the other side.

The Poem Freedom is related to The Highway Fire because the protagonist is actually dead but doesn't realize it. He has achieved freedom from the shackles of life. In so doing, he can move on and go to a better place where friends and relatives await him.

Author Biography

Mark Wilkins

A Storyteller

My name is Mark Wilkins. I am best known to my readers as A Storyteller. I pen the A Storyteller Series of Books for Love Force International Publishing. Unlike most other book series, it does not concentrate on a particular character or a particular story line. Instead, it focuses on books of short stories in various genres by a particular author, namely myself. Some of the books in the A Storyteller Book Series include serious fiction (A Week's Worth of Fiction), humorous fiction (Slices of Life) and a mixture of serious and humorous fiction and non-fiction (Classroom Confessions) and supernatural Fiction (Stories of The Supernatural).

The readers who enjoy my books like reading that sparks their imagination. They like stories with memorable and quirky characters on unusual topics. They like unexpected twists and turns in the plot. If any of these things my readers enjoy describe you, then you too will enjoy my writing.

I am comfortable writing in many different genres.

I write both humorous and serious fiction. Some of my stories are based on true events, others are totally my invention. It is up to you, the reader, to decide which stores are based on factual events and which are completely my invention because I'm not telling. I like to tell stories and I work very hard at making those stories both compelling and entertaining. I hope you enjoy reading my books.

Kindle Books by Loveforce International Publishing

Whether you are interested in true stories, fiction, humor, action, adventure, spiritual insights, quotes, poetry, self-help or children's books, Loveforce International Publishing has got you covered. **Our 99 cent commitment,** our commitment to a 99 cent (U.S.) price for all our kindle e book titles keep our books affordable. Since our books sell for the local equivalent of 99 cents (U.S.) in other global markets, people around the globe can afford them. Our books do sell all over the world. Our 99 cent commitment means there has never been a better time to stock up on books published by Love Force International! At a time when many paperbacks sell for $13.95-$17.95, our paperbacks sell for between $6.50-$7.50 (U.S.). This too is a bargain for our readers.

Many of the books listed here include their Amazon Kindle ASIN code. Typing an ASIN code into any Amazon search bar should bring that title up. If you are looking for titles published by Loveforce International Publishing you can simply type Loveforce International Publishing Company into any amazon search bar anywhere in the world and many of our books will come up. For books in Spanish type Loveforce Libros en Espanol into any Amazon search bar anywhere in the world.

Many of our books have Spanish Language versions. We didn't just slap the text onto Google Translate and pray. We worked with a professional Spanish translator born and raised in a Spanish speaking nation. We made our authors available to that person to clarify idioms and other translation glitches so that our Spanish versions are not only close to the original in meaning but they also fit within the culture(s) of Spanish Speaking nations.

We have some promotional videos for our books on Amazon Kindle. You can find many others on our You Tube channel The Loveforce International Publishing channel. Just type Loveforce International Publishing into your You Tube search bar anywhere in the world and the channel will come up along with many of our videos. Our logo is a photo of the sun coming out through a cloud over a mountain top. We have a Spanish Language You Tube Channel as well. Type Loveforce International Publishing en Espanol and you will see some of our Spanish language videos from our Loveforce enEspanol channel come up with the ones in English.

NOTE: Books with ASINs are available now the others will be available soon. All Titles are printed in English. Books with an **SP** after the title also have a version translated into Spanish. A List of Paperbacks will be below, Reader Series books with a paperback version will have **Ppr** on the same line as the title.

The Reader Series is a series of readers that are a sampling of writings by one or more authors.

The Prophet of Life Reader (7 Book Sampler) Volumes 1 & 2
What do essays, articles, stories, poetry and quotes have in common? They are all in this sampling of stories, poems and other writings from 7 of The Prophet of Life's writings found in these Kindle books.
Author: The Prophet of Life   **ISBN: 978-1-936462-07-0**
ASIN: B015D716C0 (Vol 1)   ASIN: B06XBSWKX8 (Vol 2)

The Mark Wilkins Reader 7 Book Sampler! Volumes 1 & 2
One story from seven books by Mark Wilkins. Whether its smart spouses, inquisitive fools, teachers, gangsters or ghosts these books give you a good sampling of stories by the man known throughout the world as A Storyteller. Within its pages you will find horror, humor and pathos.
 Author: Mark Wilkins   **ISBN: 978-1-936462-38-4**
ASIN: B01MU0Z51H Volume 1

The Love Force International Reader 7 Book Sampler! 4 Books in This Series

Whether you want fiction, humor, children's stories, poetry or quotes these books have got all of those and more! A sampling of 7 different books by three authors offered in Kindle books published by Love Force International.
Edited by Evan Lovefire   **Vol 1 ASIN: B06XBHD9RX**
Vol 2 ASIN: B06XBMGLNK
Vol 3 ASIN: B07DCGTLKF Vol 4
ASIN: B07DP51BWG

The Love Force International Sampler, Spanish Books Edition SP Volumes 1 & 2
These books contain a sampling of 7 different books by three authors translated into Spanish. The books translated include What Faith has Taught me, Controversy, True Stories of Inspiration & General interest and Quotes about God by The Prophet of Life, Stories of The Supernatural, Slices of Life How to Become The Person You've Always Wanted by Mark Wilkins and Classic Children's Stories You've Likely Never Heard, and my first & second books of stupid little fables by Dr. Goose.
Edited by C. Gomez Vol 1 **ASIN: B06XB3RJ2K** Vol 2
ASIN:: B07F2PLVHF

The True Stories Series is a series of books which include true stories.

True Stories!   **SP**
A riveting collection of true stories. Whether you want to know about the toddler taken by a gator at a Disney Resort, an 18 year old who doesn't exist, which popular restaurant chain has a corporate mentality of public humiliation for its employees or an alarming new trend that could affect your household this book has got it all and they are all absolutely true!
Author: The Prophet of Life   **ISBN: 978-1-936462-16-2**
ASIN: B06XVSZSZ9

True Stories: Inspiration and General Interest
SP
What do cell phone addicts, George Orwell, birds, Paul McCartney, The Nobel Prize, Black Friday, Led Zeppelin, garbage, a pep talk, tipping, Steve Jobs, Shakespeare, inspirational thoughts and your mother have in common? They are in true stories in this book. True Stories of Inspiration & General Interest brings together stories and poems about celebrities, trends and everyday people. Sometimes surprising, always interesting, it will entertain you and give you something to think about at the same time.
Author: The Prophet of Life   **ISBN: 978-1-936462-15-5**
ASIN: B00TXWVNUC   **ASIN:** B01BBCKFZU
(Spanish Edition)

Controversy

Ppr SP

What do Caitlyn Jenner, Donald Trump, a cure for AIDS, Chinese hackers, Adolf Hitler and Global Warming have in common? They are all at the heart of a controversy and there are stories about them in this unique book that turns tabloid headlines inside out. **Author:** The Prophet of Life **ISBN: 978-1-936462-19-3 ASIN: B016MWU8NS ASIN: B01CRF3098 (Spanish Edition)**

True Stories of Crime and Punishment
SP
This book of serious crime stories is ripped from headlines all over the globe. From the family that vanished, to the 11 year old girl killed in a fight over a boy, to the prisoner who hasn't eaten in 14 years, to the severed human head found near the famous Hollywood sign these stories ripped will astound you and give you pause to think.
Author: The Prophet of Life **ISBN: 978-1-936462-17-9 ASIN: B01406YZBE ASIN: B01N10ND7S (Spanish Edition)**

Strange but True!

A collection of facts and stories about people, places and things that are strange and seem like fiction but are absolutely true!

Author: Mark Wilkins **ASIN:**

The A Storyteller Series is a unique book series. Instead of concentrating on a particular character or genre, the series consists of collections of short stories by Author Mark Wilkins, Also Known As A Storyteller.

The Slice of Life Series are books with humorous stories.

Slices of Life Volume 1
SP

is a collection of humorous short stories about life. Most of them deal with marriage and family members. From smart spouses to intelligent little children to guys trying to impress their friends and in-laws trying to master technology each story is like a little slice of life but together, they make up an irresistible pie. Sit back, grab a cup of coffee and enjoy some slices of lie because, before you know it, you will have finished the whole thing. **Author:** Mark Wilkins **ISBN: 978-1-936462-11-7 ASIN: B014ZF5VY0   ASIN: B01BBBZUL0 (Spanish Edition)**

Slices of Life Volume 2
SP

This sequel to Slices of Life has more humorous stories about the rich, the poor and the middle class. It even has a story about one of their pets. Ignorance is the main theme of this book, ignorance that has consequences that are sometimes touching but always humorous. So brew so coffee or tea, sit down and relax and enjoy another satisfying batch of more slice of life because, before you know it, you will have devoured the whole thing.

Author: Mark Wilkins **ISBN: 978-1-936462-12-4 ASIN: B01M2B3YZ1 ASIN: B06XKP5C66 (Spanish Edition)**

The Stories of The Supernatural Series are books with scary stories that cross the spectrum of Horror, Occult, Ghost, Monster and Fantasy genres.

Stories of The Supernatural Volume 1
SP
Ghosts, demonic creatures, and Death. This collection of Short Stories will haunt and entertain you. Whether it's the classic evil of A Lump of Coal or the whimsy of A Ghost in the House this collection of Short Stories and poems will haunt, thrill and entertain you.
Author: Mark Wilkins **ISBN:** 978-1-936462-18-6
ASIN: B01M1N1QR5 ASIN: B01MA12YXY (Spanish Edition)

Stories of The Supernatural Volume 2
SP
In this sequel to Stories of The Supernatural there are more Ghosts, Demonic Creatures and Death. This collection of short stories Centers of Ghosts and Monsters. Within its pages you will marvel at the exploits of The Soul Collector, Shudder at the mention of the dreaded Bungadun and of the Hell Banger and ride the rails on the ghost train. Strap on your seat belts, it's going to be a bumpy ride! **Author:** Mark Wilkins **ISBN: 978-1-936462-26-1**
ASIN: B01MDJMSUY ASIN: B01M4FXDL1 (Spanish Edition)

A Storyteller Series Continued...
The A Week's Worth of Fiction Series is a series of books with seven stories of fiction each. Each book has stories organized by a particular theme. In a unique twist, each story is followed by a poem which has something indirectly to do with the story that came before it. Readers are asked to read one story and poem that follows it per day. This gives them one day to see how the story resonates with them and try and figure out how the poem is related to the story. To end the suspense, the author includes a section called "How the Poems in this Book are related to the Stories" at the end of the book.

A Week's Worth of Fiction Volume 1
SP
In Volume 1 of A Week's Worth of Fiction, People on The Edge, you will meet people on the edges of society. A security guard who struggles with a dying wife, an elderly man whose cast aside and left to die, one woman struggling to capture romance before her beauty fades and another struggling with cancer. You will meet a little boy who terrorizes a grocery store, a teenage boy searching for love and a small businessman struggling against a monopoly. If you want fictional stories you will never forget you only need to count to 7. **Author:** Mark Wilkins **ISBN: 978-1-936462-13-1**
ASIN: B01521SQ02 ASIN: B06XVD21PM (Spanish Edition)

A Week's Worth of Fiction Volume 2
SP

Volume 2 of A Week's Worth of Fiction, Science Fiction you will be intrigued and astounded by stories about a girl who has the cure for a deadly disease, a woman on a date with psycho somatic disease called prophecy, a robot chicken, a supernatural fly, an astral projection, a teacher in a new job where everything is not what it seems and a futuristic world where the only economy is barter. If you want science fiction stories you will never forget you only need to count to 7. **Author:** Mark Wilkins
ISBN: 978-1-936462-14-8 **ASIN:** B01LX9RZH7
ASIN: B071GCYFK6 **(Spanish Edition)**

A Week's Worth of Fiction Volume 3
SP

A Week's Worth of Fiction Volume 3, The Many Sides of Violence, features 7 fictional stories that explore violence. One story looks at what goes through the mind of a terrorist about to blow himself up. Another, looks at an executive considering suicide. The plots of other stories include a, man trying to outwit an armed carjacker, a sky marshal trying to figure out which passage is a terrorist, a soldier who realizes someone in his platoon is a serial killer, an ex-convict who has to decide if he should use violence to combat evil and an everyman who becomes a hero through unspeakable violence, if you want violent stories you will never forget you only need to count to 7.**Author:** Mark Wilkins
ASIN: B071WNC6ZX   **ASIN: B072K6J9HN**
(Spanish Edition)

A Week's Worth of Fiction Volume 4
SP

In A Week's Worth of Fiction 4, Realizations, you will meet people from various backgrounds who come to important realizations. You will meet a Doctor who comes to a realization about old age, a politician who struggles to be his own man, a rich man who reaches an epiphany after a chance encounter at a store, A farmer in need of help, A little boy who struggles with a new cell phone that seems processed, a swimmer who gains insight from her morning routine and a police officer who develops empathy for a hardcore gangster. If you want the fictional stories you will never forget you only need to count to 7. **Author:** Mark Wilkins **ASIN: B07217QL6H** **ASIN: B071JVQQ96** **(Spanish Edition)**

A Storyteller series continued...

The Classroom Confessions Series is a series of books with stories from the front line of public education. Stories and song lyrics mostly focus on students and teachers. Some will make you laugh, others will make you cry but they will all give you insights into public education and entertain you while giving you something to think about.

Classroom Confessions Volume 1
        SP
is a series of true stories from the front lines of public education. Within its pages you will meet quirky characters, the good, the bad and the over caffeinated. Some of them are teachers, some students and some are administrators. Some will make you laugh, others will make you cry but they all play an important role in public education. Their stories are written in way that will entertain you and give you something to think about.
Author: Mark Wilkins **ISBN: 978-1-936462-08-7**
ASIN: B00VNFJBX8   ASIN: B01MSV4N92
(Spanish Edition)

Classroom Confessions Volume 2
                SP

Is another series of true stories from the front lines of public education. Within its pages you will meet unforgettable characters like the French Substitute, Mr. Happyhands, Harry Winkwater, The Bushwhacker and of course, Julian. Some will touch your heart, others will give you something to think about but they will all entertain you. **Author:** Mark Wilkins **ASIN: B01N1OCRVC ASIN: B06XC9HDQV (Spanish Edition)**

The Love Force Novella Series: These are short novels of varying length.

Karma   Ppr   SP

The story of one man who negotiates between two different cultures, and opposing life views competing for his attention. His conflicts and struggles are overshadowed by cosmic forces he cannot understand. Karma provides insights into the struggles and conflicts we all face. **Author: Mark Wilkins**

ASIN: B0722R448R   (English Edition) ASIN: B072Z6L36 (Spanish Edition)

The Beyond Faith Series

Is a series of books that look at life from a spiritual perspective. No matter what your faith, you will find spiritual insights in these books that will enrich your life.

What Faith Has Taught Me
SP

 I am just an ordinary person who has been privileged to have a life filled with miracles and revelations. There are many times when I had nothing except faith but faith was all I needed to sustain me. My faith and my God have taught me many life lessons. This book shares some of the things my faith has taught me and the spiritual insights I have gained because of my faith. **Author:** The Prophet of Life **ISBN: 978-1-936462-03-2 ASIN: B01527IKT8 ASIN: B01EE3QSW2 (Spanish Edition)**

Finding God in A Chaotic World   SP
The world can seem so chaotic these days. Many people long for guidance. Many others want to get closer to God. How do you find God amidst the chaos and confusion? How can you discern God's messages from the multi-media blitz we are each bombarded with every day? Some people are part of an organized religion. Others are spiritual without a particular religion. Some are still searching, All of them trying to find God.

In this book, you will learn that The Lord communicates with how The Lord communicates with you. You will learn about the True Nature of God and realize just how profound God's Love and reach are. You will learn the secret of why God's will always prevails. If you are ready for revelations that may change the way you look at life in general and your life in particular, read this book.
Author: The Prophet of Life **ISBN: 978-1-936462-01-8**
ASIN: B00SLLZAAU
ASIN: B0793KDYX3 (Spanish Edition)

Finding God without Religion **SP**
People of faith are not exclusive to religion. There are many who are spiritual or agnostic. They don't fit into the doctrine, rituals and congregational community of religion. In this wisdom filled volume, people of faith but without an organized religion can gain insights into life, the afterlife and God without being brow beaten or guilt tripped into conversion. This volume is Book 2 of the Revelations of 2012 Beyond Faith series. Part 1 is entitled Finding God in A Chaotic World.
Author: The Prophet of Life **ISBN: 978-1-936462-10-0**
ASIN: B00XKPD86K **ASIN: B07F5MTFVQ**
(Spanish Edition)

Inspiration For All 1
SP

Selected Inspirational Writings. Whether you are of faith or just in need of inspiration in your life, this book full of inspirational stories, poems and essays will sustain and strengthen you on your journey. **Authors: The Prophet of Life & Mark Wilkins ASIN: B071ZM17V6 ASIN: B071JW8XXH (Spanish Edition)**

Inspiration for All 2
          SP
This is a book of selected inspirational writings by three different authors. It will not only entertain you but will also stimulate your mind by offering you alternative ways of looking at things and opportunities to gain insights. **Authors**: Mark Wilkins, The Prophet of Life & Dr. Goose. **ASIN: B0736JH6M9   ASIN: B072WK9JBH (Spanish Edition)**

Outrageous Humor Series
Books of stories and fake news articles for those with an off-beat sense of humor.

Outrageous Stories   **SP**
This book is filled with offbeat humor articles. All of them are fictitious and many of them completely outrageous. No one is safe from being made fun of be they terrorists, Presidents, Dictators, The Movie and Record Business or couch potatoes. If you are college age or older and have an offbeat, irreverent, sense of humor, this book is for you!
Author: Mark Wilkins **ISBN: 978-1-936462-33-9**
ASIN: B01LY3VZJR
ASIN: B07D1RH9W3 (Spanish Edition)

More Outrageous Stories   **SP**
This book is filled with more offbeat humor articles. All of them are fictitious and many of them completely outrageous. No one is safe from being made fun of be they terrorists, Racists, National Holidays or the medical establishment. If you are college age or older and have an offbeat, irreverent, sense of humor, this book is for you!
Author: Mark Wilkins **ISBN: 978-1-936462-33-9**
ASIN: B074Y8LTTJ

Self Help Series
This consists of books by different authors designed to help people improve their lives.

Become The Person You've Always Wanted to Be
SP

This self-help book offers a simple, yet profound method of making positive changes in your life. It includes a link to download exclusive, helpful companion worksheets to help you become the person you have always wanted to be.
Author: Mark Wilkins **ISBN: 978-1-936462-39-1**
ASIN: B01MSYVAB6   ASIN:
 B01MSYVU6R   **(Spanish Edition)**

Life Success Kit   **SP**
Spiritual Thought Leader The Prophet of Life helps you clarify what success really means to you through a series of inspirational life lessons designed to give you new perspectives on achieving success and a blueprint for making changes in the things that are preventing you from becoming a success.
Author: The Prophet of Life **ASIN: B01MZ2TSCP**
    ASIN: B078JZGWDH (Spanish Edition)

The Your Life in Rhyme Poetry Series
Is a series of Poetry books unlike any you have ever read
whether it is an exploration of life itself through a thematic
chapter on each of the various stages of life as in
Reflections in The Mirror of Life, The mixture of thought
provoking essays and inspirational poetry of Black in
America or the exploration of a single topic as in Romance
Returns or Life in Verse. The books in this series will have
you rediscovering poetry in a way that will make you
wonder why you ever avoided it in the first place.

Reflections in the Mirror of Life
This unique book explores life through its harsh realities,
pleasant diversions and positive possibilities. The book
looks at modern society, the problems it faces, and the
people who are a part of it. In a unique twist that's different
from most books of poetry, Reflections is divided into five
chapters, each of which explores a different theme woven
into the fabric of modern life. The tone for each chapter is
set by a free verse poem which is followed by a series of
rhyming poems on that theme.
Author: The Prophet of Life **ISBN: 978-1-936462-04-9
ASIN: B00V2TSAXC**

Black in America

is an exploration of racism through essays and poems. It spans from the beginnings of the Civil Rights movement through today. It looks at people who have been lightning rods for race relations in America and has some surprising insights into the people and events that have shaped race relations in America for the past 60 years. This book is a good companion for anyone who wants to gain insight into the Civil Rights movement, race relations and racism itself.   **Author:** The Prophet of Life
ISBN: 978-1-936462-09-4   ASIN: B00S05QSXA

Every Lyric Tells A Story   SP
* A collection of unique song lyrics that tell compelling stories about people, their lives, their hopes and dreams. You can find yourself and people you know in many of them. **Authors:** The Prophet of Life & Mark Wilkins   **ASIN: B01NAFDWZW**
ASIN: B07F5N1Y5G (Spanish Edition)

Romance Lives!
Romance Lives is a very special collection of Romantic Love Poems. The poems are arranged to follow the arc of a romance from its early, puppy love stages through its sweet seductions and the blissful wisdom of mature love. If you are searching for Romance in your love relationship or just want some joyful, insightful romantic reading this book is for you! **Authors: The Prophet of Life & Mark Wilkins ASIN: B07D9WY6V5**
ASIN: B07DP7HX9P (Spanish Edition)

Life in Verse

A collection of poems about life. The poems and song lyrics are about people, their lives, their hopes and dreams. You can find yourself and people you know in many of them. **Author:** The Prophet of Life **ASIN:**

The Best Quotes quotation series
Is a series of books filled with quotes attributed to the
Prophet of Life whose quotes have been used by charities,
corporations, institutions of Medicine and higher learning.
The book includes a license to use any of the quotes as
long as they are attributed to The Prophet of Life.

The Best Quotes About God   **SP**
This short book is filled with some of the more popular
quotes about God attributed to The Prophet of Life. It is
both thought provoking and inspirational. It is filled with
dozens of quotes about God that one can read and copy for
personal use.   **Author:** The Prophet of Life **ISBN: 978-
1-936462-20-9 ASIN: B018P0M8OC   ASIN:
B01BJXYHLY (Spanish Edition)**

The Best Quotes on General Subjects
    SP
This short book is filled with some of the more popular
quotes on general subjects attributed to The Prophet of
Life. The book includes quotes on topics such as life, love,
happiness, crime and punishment, wellness and includes
many of the humorous quotes attributed to The Prophet of
Life. You will find the wit and wisdom in its pages thought
provoking and inspirational. It is filled with dozens of
quotes about God that one can read and copy for personal
use.

Author: The Prophet of Life   ASIN: B01M58L9LW
ASIN: B01M58L9LW (Spanish Edition)

The Best Spiritual Quotes
SP
This book is filled with some of the more popular quotes
on Spiritual Subjects attributed to The Prophet of Life.
Included are quotes on faith, mercy, life lessons, humanity
and spirituality. You should find them to be profound,
thought provoking and inspirational. It is filled with many
pages of quotes that one can read and copy for personal
use. **Author:** The Prophet of Life
ASIN: B01MQVA87Q   **ASIN: B07DP68YSF**
(Spanish Edition)

Children's Storybook Series
All books are by Dr. Goose who writes in both prose and rhyming verse.

Classic Children's Stories You've Likely Never Heard SP
Help develop your child's creative abilities and develop their imagination by reading them stories from this book that has no illustrations. Whether it's a story about Prince trying to find the answer to a question, a spider talking about a savior, a kingdom in trouble or a child trying to save the world you will find yourself wanting to read these children's stories with international flavor again and again. This first book in the series is for smaller children.
Author: Dr. Goose **ISBN:** 978-1-936462-40-7
ASIN: B01NAF8QNU   **ASIN:**
B01MR5PR84   **(Spanish Edition)**

More Classic Children's Stories You've Likely Never Heard   SP
This sequel gives you more unknown classics. The book introduces new characters like a little chicken whose life is similar to a person's and a ballad about a hairy man. There is a story about a prince whose refusal causes an international incident. There is even an updated version of classic children's story everyone knows from different character's points of view. This second book in the series helps tweens and juvenile children creative abilities and develop their imagination as stories from this book that has no illustrations either. **Author:** Dr. Goose **ISBN:** 978-1-936462-41-4

ASIN: B074Y8G4JZ ASIN:
B0755YK6NH   (Spanish Edition)

My First Book of Stupid Little Fables SP
Whether the greed of mooches and lunch thieves, sadistic children, or bizarre stories about pets this first installment in the series of irreverently humorous stories with twisted endings about the selfish and the greedy delivers. It even has the stupid little drawings! For Juveniles. **Author:** Dr. Goose
ISBN: 978-1-936462-44-5   ASIN: B07FFCNCQZ
ASIN: B07FFF13N4 (Spanish Edition)

My Second Book of Stupid Little Fables SP
Whether it's well-meaning but incompetent grandmas, egotistical women, sadistic children, or crazy people in shopping centers, this second installment in the series of irreverently humorous stories with twisted endings about the selfish and the greedy delivers. It even has the drawings you love to make fun of just like the first one! For Juveniles. **Author:** Dr. Goose   **ISBN:**
ASIN: **ASIN:** **(Spanish Edition)**

More Children's Stories
School Kidz Volume 1 Elementary and Middle School SP
Six funny stories about kids who are smarter than their age. Within its pages you will meet A boy whose vocabulary is better than the adults in his school, a kid who escapes a spanking, A kid who gets a new cell phone with a built in problem and a brother and sister who learn how get rid of junk from an old aunt. Recommended for kidz ages 12-16. **Author:** Mark Wilkins **ASIN: B0717B6SQ4**

ASIN: B078JMR7ZB (Spanish Edition)

School Kidz Volume 2 High School   **SP**
9 stories about kids who are in high school. Within its pages you will meet a group of Kidz who get involved in a rotten egg war, a girl who doesn't exist, and a kid who sends a friend on a date with his sister. Recommended for kidz ages 14-18. **Author:** Mark Wilkins **ASIN: B071W5WZZN**

Coming Soon E Workbooks and an E Textbook!

A series of mini and one comprehensive E Textbook Under the title of Mr. Wilkins Teaches English by Mark Wilkins

The specific mini textbooks will be on topics such as Reading and Responding to Literature, and Methods for Writing Paragraphs and Essays. The Comprehensive text will include a weekly spelling component and both the mini texts and comprehensive Text will include creative lessons that promote creativity and critical thinking in students while fitting into common core standards. The mini texts will be no more than 99 cents each and the comprehensive text will be paperback for under $10! All of the books are freshly created and contain exclusive intellectual property you won't find in any other texts. These books are perfect for students learning high school English levels 9 & 10 whether you are a classroom teacher or are home schooling your child. We are making the commitment to keep all of the books at low prices to allow parents and school districts to afford texts in the face of shrinking educational budgets. Purchasers will be given an opportunity to receive an email with a printable version of the exercises and assignments as well as links to online testing free of charge.

Author: Mark Wilkins   **ISBN:**   **ASIN:**

Compelling Stories for Adaptation to Short Film For Film Students

Compelling stories in a set location with six or less characters. Easily adaptable to screenplay with notes on adapting them.
Author: Mark Wilkins   **ISBN:**   **ASIN:**

Loveforce Paperbacks

All of our paperback books cost between $6.50 and $7.50.

Stories of The Supernatural: A Storyteller Series Book SP Loveforce Duo

This collection of 15 stories is filled with ghosts, demonic creatures, monsters and death. It will haunt you, thrill you and entertain you. Within its pages you will marvel at the exploits of The Soul Collector and the uniqueness of Life Lines and Cannibal Money. You will shudder at the mention of a lump of coal or the dreaded Bungadun of Blood Valley and ride the rails on the ghost train. Strap on your seat belts, it's going to be a bumpy ride! **Author:** Mark Wilkins

ISBN-13: 978-1936462537   ISBN-13: 978-1936462575 SP

Karma   SP

Karma is the story of one man who negotiates between two different cultures, and opposing life views competing for his attention. His conflicts and struggles are overshadowed by cosmic forces he cannot understand. Karma provides insights into the struggles and conflicts we all face.

Author: Mark Wilkins   **ISBN-13: 978-1936462506**
ISBN-13: 978-1936462582 SP

A Week's Worth of Fiction Volumes 1 & 2
SP   Loveforce Duo

Whether it's people on the edges of society or Science Fiction Stories, this collection of Volumes 1 & 2 of A Week's Worth of Fiction gives you 2 volumes each with 7 stories that will thrill you, surprise you and make you think. Often dystopic and sometimes surreal, if you want stories you will never forget you only need to count to 7 and you can do it twice in this special paperback edition.

Author: Mark Wilkins   **ISBN-13: 978-1936462551**

Totally Outrageous Stories! Outrageous Satire
Loveforce Trio

There is absolutely nothing that escapes ridicule in this flagrantly outrageous, biting satire of everything you can imagine. This smart, flippant book pokes fun at the entertainment industry, the medical establishment, politics, societal norms, history and science. If you want to laugh to humor with no mercy, you have to get totally outrageous!
Author: Mark Wilkins   **ISBN-10:** 1936462494   **ISBN-13:** 978-1936462490

Slices of Life: Stories of Humor and Pathos (A Storyteller Series)   SP Loveforce Duo

Slices of Life Slices is a collection of humorous short stories about life. Most of them deal with marriage and family members. There are smart spouses, intelligent little children, guys trying to impress their friends and in-laws trying to master technology. Ignorance is the main theme of this book, ignorance that has consequences that are sometimes touching but always humorous. Each story is like a little slice of life but together, they make up an irresistible pie. Sit back, grab a cup of coffee and enjoy some slices of life because, before you know it, you will have finished the whole thing.
Author: Mark Wilkins   **ISBN-13: 978-1936462452**
ISBN-13: 978-1936462469 SP

Public School Confessions: Stories From The Front Lines of Public Education Loveforce Duo SP

Teachers, students and administrators come to life and often clash in dozens of stories from the front lines of public education. Within these pages you will meet people who are smart, rebellious and over caffeinated. Some stories will make you laugh, some will make you cry but they will also entertain you and make you think. **Author:** Mark Wilkins **ISBN-13: 978-1936462056   ISBN-13: 978-1936462063 SP**

The Faith Trilogy   SP   Loveforce Trio

•   This Faith Trilogy Paperback includes three faith filled books: What Faith Has Taught Me, The Best Quotes About God and Inspiration for All: Selected Inspirational Writings. **Author:** Mark Wilkins **ISBN-13: 978-1936462513   ISBN-13: 978-1936462520 (Spanish Edition)**

The Agnostic Faith Trilogy   SP   Loveforce Trio
Three great books combined in one paperback book! You get: Finding God without Religion, The Best Spiritual Quotes and Finding god in a Chaotic World. **Author:** The Prophet of Life
ISBN-13: 978-1936462476   ISBN-13: 978-1936462599 (Spanish Edition)

Black in America
Black in America is an exploration of racism in America through essays and poems. It spans from the beginnings of the civil rights movement through today, It includes powerful new poems "Why We Say Black Lives Matter", "Baltimore", "Requiem for Laquan" It takes a look at people who have been lightning rods for race relations in America and has some surprising insights into the people and events that have shaped race relations in America for the past 60 years. It is a powerful work that teaches as it entertains and allows the reader gain new insights.
Author: The Prophet of Life
ISBN-13: 978-1936462025

Controversies
    SP

What do Caitlyn Jenner, Donald Trump, Hollywood Sex Scandals, a cure for AIDS, Chinese hackers, Adolf Hitler and Global Warming have in common? They are all at the heart of a controversy and there are stories about them in this unique book that turns tabloid headlines inside out.

Author: Mark Wilkins **ISBN-13: 978-1936462483**

www.ingramcontent.com/pod-product-compliance
Lightning Source LLC
Chambersburg PA
CBHW022202170626
46807CB00005B/2308